Happy Endings
Are All Alike

Happy Endings Are All Alike

A novel by
Sandra Scoppettone

Boston • Alyson Publications, Inc.

Grateful acknowledgment is made to Norma Millay
Ellis for permission to reprint two lines from "The
Goose Girl" by Edna St. Vincent Millay from
Collected Poems, Harper & Row. Copyright 1923,
1951 by Edna St. Vincent Millay and Norma Millay
Ellis.

This is a trade paperback by Alyson Publications,
40 Plympton St., Boston, Mass. 02118.
Distributed in the U.K. by GMP Publishers,
P.O. Box 247, London N17 9QR England.

Originally published by Harper & Row.
First Alyson edition: January 1991

Library of Congress Cataloging-in-Publication Data
Scoppettone, Sandra.
     Happy endings are all alike.

     SUMMARY: Small town prejudices emerge when a
love affair between two teenage girls is revealed.
     [1. Lesbians—Fiction. 2. Rape—Fiction.
3. Prejudices] I. Title.
PZ7.S4136Hap   [Fic]   78-2976
ISBN 1-55583-177-X

For my editor, Liz Gordon,
who helped to make many dreams come true

I

Even though Jaret Tyler had no guilt or shame about her love affair with Peggy Danziger she knew there were plenty of people in this world who would put it down. Especially in a small town like Gardener's Point, a hundred miles from New York City. She and Peggy didn't go around wearing banners, but there were some people who knew.

Like Jaret's mother, Kay. Of course, Kay was an unusual woman, particularly for Gardener's Point. But even though Jaret and Kay were open and honest with each other, Jaret wasn't sure she would have told her about Peggy if Kay hadn't found out for herself. Sometimes Jaret still remembered that day and the

1

first wave of shock when, over breakfast, Kay said:

"So, would Cree Cree like more bacon?"

Oh, wow! Obviously, Kay knew. What would happen now? Whatever it was, Jaret decided before saying anything, she was not going to give up Peggy . . . ever.

"What do you mean?" she asked, stalling.

"I mean," Kay said, lighting her fifth cigarette of the morning, "I know."

"Know?"

"Oh, Jaret, please."

Jaret waved the smoke away and tried swallowing her homemade granola, which felt like shotgun pellets in her mouth.

"Sorry," Kay said, making a fan with her napkin.

"I wish you wouldn't smoke so much."

"Don't try and change the subject. I know about Cree Cree and Char."

"*Ch*ar," she said automatically, pronouncing the *ch* as in *charge*.

"All right. *Ch*ar. Honestly, Jaret, couldn't you do any better?"

Jaret wanted to die from embarrassment. They had gotten the names from a dumb movie called *Home in Indiana* made in the forties. They had watched it on a rainy Saturday afternoon and rolled on the floor laughing over it. This really insipid actress named Jeanne Crain was Char and somebody else named

2

June Haver was Cree Cree and an awful goony boy named Lon McCallister was Sparky. The whole thing had just broken them up and from then on they'd started calling each other those names. Jaret was Cree Cree and Peggy was Char. And Jaret knew she would never have told her mother about their private names for each other even if she'd chosen to tell her about their love affair. Some things you just didn't tell anyone. The only way her mother could have known about the nicknames was to have read Peggy's love letters; love letters Jaret kept hidden in the back of her sock drawer.

"You creep," she said, "you read them."

"I was wondering when you'd realize that." Kay ran a hand through her black curly hair, something she always did when she was nervous. "What can I say, kid? I'm guilty. I didn't mean to. . . . Well, I did mean to once I saw them. There's no point in pretending they jumped into my hands and etched their words on my eyeballs by themselves, is there?"

"No, there isn't."

"No, I didn't think so. But I wasn't snooping— honest, Jare."

"You just wanted a pair of my socks to wear on your ears, right?"

"You're not going to believe this," Kay said, stubbing out her cigarette.

"Try me."

3

"I was looking for my Q-tips."

"You know what, Mom? You're right—I don't believe you."

"It's true . . . really."

Jaret stared at her, waiting to see if her mouth twitched to the right. If it did, she was lying. Foolproof evidence. Jaret counted to ten and Kay's full mouth stayed quiet. Innocent.

"Okay, I believe you. But what made you look in my sock drawer for the Q-tips?"

"I looked everywhere. . . . I thought I'd go mad." She poured a cup of coffee, offered another one to Jaret, who refused. "I finally found them. In the medicine cabinet," she said sheepishly.

"Oh, Mom."

"It is definitely a conspiracy. The inanimate objects in the world are trying to take over. They do it all the time. You know that."

Jaret nodded. She'd heard this tirade before. It was one of Kay's favorite theories.

"You put a pencil down, turn around for a second, look back and it's gone. Gone! You spend five, ten minutes looking where you put it, turn around again, look back and there it is! It's their plot to drive humans crazy."

"Mom, I know about that plot," Jaret said patiently. "Do you want to talk about the letters or not?"

4

"I do. Look, first let me say that I'm sorry I read them—I mean, I know I violated your space and all that but I'm human. At least if they'd been in envelopes I wouldn't have seen the salutation. I never would have opened an envelope, Jaret. You know that, don't you?"

"I suppose, but that doesn't make it any better, Mom."

"I know. I just thought I'd try. Well, anyway, I saw this bunch of papers and one sort of fell open and there was this 'Dear, sweet Cree Cree.' I mean, come on, kid, who could resist?"

"An honorable, decent, mature person."

"Right." She shrugged. "I guess that leaves me out."

"But it doesn't, Mom. You've always been that. That's why I've always liked you."

"Thanks. I'm sorry I failed you. I couldn't help it. I had to know."

"Okay, okay. So now you know. Just *what* do you know?" Jaret quickly began to calculate whether she would admit to everything or not.

"For openers, I know that Char is Peggy Danziger."

"And?"

Kay took a cigarette from her pack, made big flourishes tapping it, even though it was filtered, struck a match which fizzled, struck another which worked and then took a long drag. "I guess I know that you're . . ." She gestured futilely. "Are you?"

5

"Am I what?" Jaret certainly wasn't going to beat around the bush if they were going to talk about it.

"I mean, Jaret, are you and Peggy . . . you know?"

"Yes, I *do* know. What we're trying to find out here is if *you* know."

"Are you a lawyer, or what?"

"Not yet." Someday she would be—no question.

"Oh, God! Are you and Peggy lovers?"

"Yes." There.

They stared at each other for a few seconds and then Kay looked away, down at the congealing remains of egg on her plate. Finally she mumbled, "Why, Jaret?"

Jaret had expected all kinds of questions but never "Why?" What did that even mean? It really bugged her.

"You know, Mom, sometimes you're really a V.I.P." She stood up abruptly, knocking over her chair, and left the room.

Kay knew that V.I.P. stood for Very Immature Person.

Jaret had spent that day feeling sick to her stomach, not knowing what would happen, wondering if her mother would tell her father, wondering if she'd be sent to her Aunt Sandy's in Texas for the summer. In two months she and Peggy would graduate; in the fall she would go to Radcliffe, Peggy to Smith. They wouldn't see each other much then. Sure, there would be weekends, holidays, but it wouldn't be the same. So they'd planned to spend every possible moment of the summer together. Peggy, because of her bout with mononucleosis that spring, wasn't planning to work. Jaret, who had saved a lot of money from past summer jobs, convinced her parents that since college was such a big project, such heavy stuff, she needed the vacation; it would be good to make the transition that way. It was a super time to look forward to. And now she wondered if her life was over.

Later that night Kay came into her room. She turned the desk chair around and sat down, leaning her chin on her arm, which rested on the chair back. Jaret thought she looked like a kid, the outfit of overalls and work shirt helping to complete the picture. Neither of them said anything for a moment or two and Jaret twisted her long brown hair around a finger while she waited. Then Kay smiled.

"You know what, kid? You're absolutely right. Sometimes I'm definitely a V.I.P. But only sometimes."

Jaret smiled back, both dimples prominent. "Right."

"I just gotta ask some questions."

"Shoot."

"I feel awkward." She lit a cigarette and took a

7

small ashtray out of her back pocket. "You know what I mean?"

"Sure. I know it's not considered normal and all that. I'm not dumb, you know."

"Oh, kid, *that* I know. Okay. Are you happy in this . . . this relationship? God, I hate that word. I mean, it's a perfectly good word but Lord, what they've done to it. Anway, I don't have a substitute. So, are you? I mean *really* happy, Jare?"

"I *really* am, Mom."

"What about boys?"

"Nothing. They do nothing for me. I tried but, well, when I kiss a boy it's like kissing a piece of white bread. When I kiss Peggy I feel all tingly."

Kay took a couple of quick drags on her cigarette and looked at the floor.

"I'm sorry," Jaret said, recognizing her mother's embarrassment. "I guess you don't want to hear stuff like that."

"The hell with what I *want* to hear."

"I mean, what it is is girls, sí, boys, no. I know it's heavy, Mom, but I just can't help it."

"What happened with Peter? He seemed like a real nice guy."

"He is a nice guy. It's got nothing to do with him. It's not his fault. It's me. I don't mean that it's my *fault*; it's just that I'm different, I guess. I mean, I know life would be easier if I was like everyone

8

else . . . but that's just not the way it is."

"I suppose I shouldn't ask if you did anything more with Peter than kiss?" Kay's hand made a quick path through her hair.

"No, you shouldn't." The idea of discussing her sex life in any form with her mother did not appeal to Jaret. Still, she understood why Kay was asking. "Look, I know where you're coming from, Mom, but don't let it freak you out. I'll tell you this: Whatever I did with boys I found really boring. I didn't get turned on, okay?"

"I got it," Kay said.

"And it's got nothing to do with you and Dad. I mean, you didn't make some horrible mistake in raising me or anything. And it's not so terrible. In fact, it's pretty nice. So don't lay a guilt trip on yourself, okay?"

"Okay."

"Good. What else?"

Kay chewed on her lip for a second and then shrugged. "I guess nothing right now. If you're happy that's all that counts."

Jaret smiled. "That's what we think, Peggy and I. As long as we're happy, right?"

"Right. I like Peggy, you know. I think she's a good kid."

"I'm glad."

Kay stood up and replaced the chair at the desk.

9

"Are you going to tell Dad?"

"Not right now, okay? Let me digest it first." She leaned down and kissed Jaret lightly on the cheek. "Get some sleep."

"I just want to say one thing, Mom."

"What?"

"I know you probably think this is a phase but I think you should know that I'm sure it's not. I think you should know that."

Kay nodded, smiled. "Thanks for telling me." Just before she closed the door she poked her head back in. "Jare, when we were first married your father and I called each other Puppy and Poochie. Good night, kid."

Now it was two months later, the summer stretched ahead of Jaret and Peggy, and still Kay had not told Bert, Jaret's father. Well, maybe that was best. Lesbianism was a hard thing for men to understand, Jaret thought. There were times when she was sure that Chris, her brother, knew and other times she was sure he didn't. He wasn't easy to read because he was not communicating with the family these days. But there was plenty of time for change. After all, he was only fifteen.

The other two people who knew were Bianca Chambers, her best friend after Peggy, and Peggy's sister, Claire, who was always threatening to tell everyone. It was lousy to have that hanging over their heads because they could imagine what would happen in Gardener's Point if it were ever made public. And they were right.

2

Peggy Danziger's mother was dead. She had died in
December, three days before Christmas. Dr. Thomas
Danziger, Peggy's father, refused to go to the funeral
and locked himself in his room for nine days. On the
tenth his sister, Paula, sat in the hall on the floor for
two and a half hours and talked to him through the
closed door. Finally he came out, looking terrible. He
had a scraggly beard and he hadn't bathed or changed
his clothes, so you could smell him when he walked
by. Paula led him into the bathroom, stripped him
down to his shorts, turned on the shower and ordered
him into it, closing the door behind her. When he
emerged from the bathroom he was shaved, dressed

in a neat, clean outfit and, though he'd lost weight, he was still rather round. From then on he made an effort, although anyone who looked closely could see that a light had gone out of his eyes.

Claire had never gotten along with her mother, but often said she had "great respect for her even though I cannot agree with her ideologically." When Mrs. Danziger died Claire was in her junior year at college. She insisted on leaving school until Peggy graduated, even though her father could easily have afforded a housekeeper. And even though Peggy was almost eighteen.

Claire had a dim view of herself. She was very intelligent but she was definitely not pretty. She had been a shock to friends and relatives, particularly when they saw her beside Peggy. They would say things like:

"Oh, what a beautiful little girl you are, Peggy. Just look at that gorgeous blond hair and those big green eyes." Then: "And this must be Claire."

The truth was that Claire was quite homely. But not in her mother's eyes. Never. And she always tried to make Claire feel lovely. Claire, not buying the "inner beauty" pitch, resented her mother for the effort and for her own good looks. It was a world where "pretty" counted; in commercials, print ads, the movies, television, looks were everything. And no matter what her mother, the Women's Movement, or *Ms.*

magazine told her, Claire still felt homely and hopeless. No man, she was convinced, would ever want her, and although she believed that there were other things in life, having love, husband, children, was tops in her book.

Her parents tried to explain that what came from inside her was what kept boys and men away, not how she looked. She did not believe them. So when her mother died Claire took the opportunity to be mistress of a household. She would have nine months of running the house on Prospect Street, of being in charge, playing Mother, even Wife. She might never have the chance again and she'd be damned if she'd miss it!

Peggy and her mother had been extremely close, adoring each other, enjoying the same things. People seeing them together often thought they were sisters. They exchanged ideas, gossiped, laughed. When Erica died Peggy was struck numb. And then she developed mononucleosis. Everyone said it was psychosomatic. Even so, the tests said she had it and she had to stay home from school. Claire was elated.

"You see, Daddy, you see. It's a good thing I left school. I would have had to anyway, wouldn't I?"

"Yes, Claire."

"I mean, who would take care of her if I were at school? I ask you, who would be here to take care of her if I hadn't left school? I was right all along, wasn't I?"

"Yes, Claire."

Peggy was depressed by her mother's absence and Claire's presence. If Claire hadn't been there Peggy felt she probably would have been able to deal with her grief. But Claire wouldn't allow it.

"Come on now, upward and onward. You can't sulk forever."

"I'm not sulking, Claire."

"Well, we can't have depression. Put a smile on that pretty face."

"I don't feel like smiling."

"Well, why not?"

"My mother died."

"Oh, honestly."

When Peggy became ill in February, Claire changed her tactics, but not for the better.

"Now you just take it easy, Baby, and I'll take care of everything. I'm not going to let anything happen to my pretty, precious baby sister."

"Nothing is going to happen, Claire. I just have to rest and I'll get rid of this gazinga."

"I'll just plump up these pillows for you, Baby, and make the darling more comfy."

"The pillows are fine."

"Would you like some juice, honey? Got to drink your juice, you know."

"I don't have to push fluids, Claire—this isn't a cold or a flu."

"How about some nice hot tea?"

"How about shutting up?"

"You little ingrate."

When Bianca Chambers first suggested bringing Jaret Tyler over, Peggy said no.

Bianca threw back her head and spread her arms as though nailed to a cross. "But why not, my dar-ling? Why not, I ask? Jaret is a fun person. Why do you persist in this way? It cuts me to the quick."

"I'm sorry about your quick but I just don't like her."

"You'll be the death of me," she said and threw herself into a wing chair, moving it at least three inches. Bianca was very big, almost six feet tall, and her body was literally shaped like a pear. The worst thing was that her head was much too small for her body, so she'd taken to wearing her frizzy light-brown hair au naturel, which meant that it stood straight out at all angles. But at least it gave the impression that her head matched her body. She had a very nice face: beautiful blue eyes and a good straight nose. Perfect for film, she often said. Bianca intended to be an actress and to this end she directed everything.

"Pourquoi? Tell your dearest friend why you don't like this person."

"She gives me a pain in the gazinga."

"You sound like an illiterate. Do you know you use

16

that word for everything?" Bianca shoved a cigarette in her black holder.

"It's a good word."

"It tells me ab-so-lute-ly nothing."

Absently, Peggy started braiding her hair. "You remember when you tried to get us together about three years ago? Well, it didn't work."

"Jaret was a child then—we all were, my dear. Now we've matured, become . . . WOMEN."

"I guess," Peggy said. "But why is it I feel like a kid most of the time?"

"That's because you're sick and full of burning."

"What burning?"

"Never mind. Back to our little problem. You see, my dear," Bianca said, letting the smoke trail from her nostrils, "the whole thing is simply too weird for words. You are my best friend, yes, chérie? And Jaret is also my best friend. So why wouldn't you naturally *adore* one another? It stands to reason, yes?"

"It stands to reason, no."

"But why not?" Bianca asked, one arm bent at the elbow, the hand flung out.

"Well, for one thing she runs around with that humungus crowd, and our crowd's, you know, very low profile."

"So low you can barely see it. I suppose what you mean by 'our crowd' is you, me, Mary Lou and Betsy?"

"And what's wrong with that? Who says you have

17

to go around in packs of hundreds?"

"Hundreds?"

"Well, that Murchison-Auerbacher crowd seems like they have hundreds." Peggy let the braid unravel. When she had first gone to Gardener's Point High she had wanted to be a part of that crowd, but it hadn't worked out. Peggy found them silly, immature, and they didn't take to her either. She had naturally gravitated toward girls with more interests and ideas. "They're too heavy for me."

"Jaret doesn't like them much either, dear heart."

"Then why does she hang out with them?"

"Nobody else to hang out with. After all, what was she supposed to do when the big crowd from last year graduated?"

Most of Jaret's friends had been a year ahead of her and when they graduated she was left behind. Then when school started again, and Ann Murchison and Nancy Auerbacher invited her to a party, she began to go around with them.

"Well, I don't know, Bianca. She just turns me off. I'm not into all that stuff, you know."

"And what, dear heart, do you mean?" She stubbed out her cigarette, ceremoniously blew the last puff of smoke from her holder and dropped it into her shirt pocket.

"Dope and booze and stuff."

Bianca gave a long trilling laugh as though she were practicing scales. "Don't make me laugh."

18

"Seems I already did."

"Jaret doesn't even smoke cigarettes." She punctuated this with a bob of her head.

"I still don't dig her."

Bianca rose grandly, swept around the room, gesturing wildly. "All right, all right, say no more. I will not bring her here. She'll be relieved."

"What do you mean?" Peggy narrowed her eyes, insulted.

"Well, if you must have the truth she had no desire to come. She feels the same way about you but she was going to do it as a favor to me."

"Well," Peggy said, scrunching up on the couch where a makeshift bed was arranged, "what a humungus nerve!"

"*You* are simply absurd. Why on earth do you care?" Bianca returned to the chair, trying for an elegant position: one arm over the back of the wing, legs crossed, work-booted foot dangling.

"You see, that's just what I thought. Jaret Tyler thinks she's queen of the gazinga or something."

"No, she doesn't. She thinks you think you are."

"*Me?*"

"That is correct."

"*Me?*" Peggy said again, appalled. "I'm the most down-to-earth person you'd ever want to meet."

"Well, so is Jaret."

"I'll bet!"

"You want to?" Bianca patted her frizz.

19

"Want to what?"

"Bet."

"What are you talking about?"

"You know, sometimes I doubt that high I.Q. of yours. Would you like to bet that you find Jaret Tyler a very down-to-earth, fabulous person?"

"How much?"

"A Cher record."

"I hate Cher, Bianca. I think she's revolting."

"Yes, I know. You can choose who you want. I suppose you want the Beatles. So ancient."

"I *have* all their records. You can buy me a book when *I* win. The complete Edna St. Vincent Millay."

Bianca grinned.

"What's so funny?"

"She's Jaret's favorite poet too. You have a lot in common, Peggy. You'll see."

"I'll see nothing."

"Oh, you *are* trying. Anyway, I won't be able to come around as much after Monday, you know, so it would be practical to like her."

"I guess I'm supposed to ask what happens on Monday, huh?"

Bianca looked hurt. "You've forgotten. Oh well, I suppose you have other things on your mind. We begin rehearsals for *The Little Foxes.* I'm playing Regina, of course."

"Of course." Peggy kidded Bianca about her acting

20

but she also admired her and thought she was very good.

"I must fly now, dear girl. Tomorrow I'll return with Jaret and you will owe me a Cher record. You'll *adore* each other. You'll see. Ta-ta."

Bianca won her Cher record. Within ten minutes Jaret and Peggy were laughing and talking. It was true. They had many, many things in common. They were so enjoying each other, in fact, that Bianca, who sat silent on the other side of the room, experienced a momentary twinge of jealousy. But then she realized she was pleased that her two dearest friends in the world would now be best friends themselves.

3

June 23rd

Tonight was graduation. Only two more years for me, then freedom. Can't wait. You won't catch me wearing that cap and gown though—no way. They can send me the dumb diploma by carrier pigeon for all I care.

Me and the guys hung out in front of the Bee Hive and watched when the seniors came out after grad. They were all going to some club or something. Richie and Brett had the Buick really souped up. They are some dudes! Richie was with big-jugs Karen and Brett with Pam . . . per usual. That Karen . . .

I'll take some of that. Any time.

Later we ran into Pete, John and that creep Stewart. I gave the punk a couple jabs. He makes me want to puke. How can he let himself get out of shape like that? If there's one thing I hate it's fat.

When I came in, Himself was sitting watching the tube . . . some dumb movie out of the dark ages. . . . He wanted to be pals and buddies and all that crap . . . but I said I wanted to sack out. Who needs to be pals with your Old Man?

Tomorrow starts vacation. Maybe something cool will happen this summer. One thing, for sure, I'm going to get me a piece. No two ways about it.

4

"Do you know what today is?" Jaret asked.

"Two days after graduation." Peggy smiled.

"And what else?"

"June twenty-fifth."

"That's right. And what's the twenty-fifth?" She pushed a piece of Peggy's blond hair out of her eyes.

"I give up. What?"

"You have no romance in your soul."

"Yes I do and you know it."

Jaret could see Peggy's green eyes teasing her and felt relieved. She sometimes became afraid that suddenly Peggy would change her mind or lose interest or something. Not that she didn't trust Peggy. She just couldn't believe her own good luck. How was it possible that she had found someone as wonderful as Peggy to love? And be loved by?

"You *do* know what day it is, don't you?"

"Sure. How could I forget?" Peggy took Jaret's hand, kissed the fingertips, then held it. "It's been two months."

Now Jaret felt slightly foolish for thinking Peggy had forgotten.

Sensing this, Peggy said, "Don't be so insecure, Jare. I'm into this gazinga just as much as you."

"I know. But I feel like I have everything and I just don't believe any one person can. I keep waiting for some kind of zap. It always seems if you get a lucky break, if something great happens, then something lousy happens soon after."

"You mean like me getting accepted at Smith and then my mother dying?"

"Exactly."

"Yeah, you shouldn't count on anything, you know." Peggy took a long swallow of Tab. It was a device. She was tired of crying about her mother and though the pain had lessened somewhat it was still very much there. She'd learned that when she was on the verge of tears, swallowing something, moving from one spot to another or biting the insides of her cheeks stemmed the flow. The insides of her cheeks were raw and ragged. Drinking Tab was preferable.

Jaret was never fooled by these tricks. She squeezed Peggy's hand. "Want to go to the lake?"

"Too cold. Let's go to your house and take a walk in the woods."

The weather was unusually crisp for the end of June. They each put on a light jacket, started for the door. Claire, coming from the kitchen, met them in the hall. She jumped in an exaggerated fashion as though she'd stumbled onto Frankenstein's Monster and the Spider Woman.

"Oh, Claire," Peggy said with despair.

"I wasn't expecting to meet anyone."

"Anyone? You *are* hopeless."

"*I'm* hopeless? You have some nerve, Miss Priss." As always, Claire refused to look at Jaret. "And where are you going?"

"We, *Jaret* and I," she said deliberately, "are going for a walk. Want to come?" She knew Claire would not.

"No thanks. I wouldn't be caught dead." Claire turned her back and went on up the stairs.

Jaret felt depressed. It never failed. Claire's disdain for their relationship always got to her. Peggy tried to make a joke of it but Jaret knew it affected her deeply. With a single look or word, Claire could sink them into terrible agony. It didn't matter that they felt right about their love; Claire represented society and her constant put-down had an undermining effect. Jaret felt the same way now as she had the day Claire discovered them in each other's arms.

It was a month after Bianca had brought them together. Jaret spent the night, and in the morning Peggy awakened crying. It wasn't an unusual way for her to start the day then; her pain was still very fresh. Jaret put her arms around Peggy and held her close, stroked her hair, murmured comfort. As they lay in bed the door opened and they both jumped.

Claire stood in the doorway, her face turning pink, eyes narrowing behind her glasses. "Well, I . . . you . . . Just what I thought. Disgusting. I knew it. . . . I knew it."

"Knew what?" Peggy asked, trembling.

"Knew that this was a deviant relationship, that's what. I'm a psych major and I know all about these things."

"I don't know what you're talking about, Claire." It was almost true. Way in the back of Peggy's mind a small light was beginning but it was still very dim.

"Don't hand me that. Do you think I don't have eyes? Do you think I'm a jackass? I saw you."

"Saw what?"

Jaret, also quivering, stared at the ceiling. The accusation, though untrue, was not unfounded, at least not for her. She'd come to know quite clearly what she felt for Peggy, though she had never expressed it.

27

"I saw," Claire went on, her arms crossed over her breasts, "that you jumped out of each other's arms when I opened this door."

"Number one," Peggy said, anger giving her courage, "you have no right to come bursting into my room without knocking like some humungus prison guard. And number two, though it's really none of your business, I was crying and Jaret was comforting me and that's what you saw."

"Really? Then why did you jump like two guilty criminals?"

"We . . . we . . . you frightened us." She knew that wasn't the truth but she also didn't know what the truth was. Why *had* they jumped? She didn't want to go on with this. It was making her angry and uncomfortable. "I wish you'd leave, Claire."

"I'll bet you do. Well, we'll see about this when Daddy comes home tonight."

"Fine. Now just split."

"Don't worry. I'm not interested in being in the same room with a pair of perverts." She slammed the door loudly but the word "pervert" slammed into them even harder.

They lay very still, each on her own side of the bed. It was a long time before Peggy spoke.

"Are you all right, Jare?"

"I'm not sure."

Neither looked at the other.

28

"She's disgusting," Peggy said.

Jaret wondered if Peggy thought her sister was disgusting for disregarding her privacy or for making such an accusation. Since they'd become close friends, she and Peggy had talked about many things but never lesbianism. Now this suddenly seemed sinister to Jaret. Peggy was usually an open person, nonjudgmental. But perhaps for her, as for many other people, this subject was different. And perhaps Jaret had known it all along and that was why she'd never brought it up. That was why she'd never told this dear friend, someone she thought of as her other half, that for years and years she had been attracted to girls. Now she could *never* tell her.

"You mustn't let it get you," Peggy said.

When Jaret felt Peggy's hand touch hers she pulled away as though she'd been scorched, threw back the covers and jumped out of bed. "I've got to get going," she said.

Peggy sat up, leaning on an elbow. "Going? Going where?" It was Saturday and they'd planned to spend the day together.

"I have some errands . . . for my mother."

"You never said . . ."

"I just remembered."

Jaret took her clothes into Peggy's bathroom and shut the door.

Peggy was alone with her thoughts. Why *had* they

29

jumped? Why was Jaret acting so strange? Sure, what Claire said had been upsetting, but it was the kind of thing they would normally have found funny. But nothing felt funny; it felt awful. It was especially awful because Jaret was so obviously hurt. And that hurt *her*. She couldn't stand Jaret to be hurt because . . . because she *loved* Jaret. Well, what the hell was wrong with that? There was nothing wrong with two women loving each other. Nothing at all. Her mother had loved her best friend, Renee, and wasn't ashamed of it. You weren't a pervert just because you loved someone of your own sex, for God's sake!

Jaret came out of the bathroom to find Peggy standing in the middle of the room, staring at her. It made her feel naked.

"Listen, Jare, we're not perverts because we love each other. You know that, don't you? I mean, I love you, I really do. And I know you love me and so what? There's nothing wrong with that and you can't let Claire make some ugly gazinga out of it."

The final nail in the coffin, Jaret thought. If she'd had the slightest reservation about Peggy's feelings they were perfectly clear now. Lesbianism was ugly to her.

"Jare, do you hear me? Loving each other does not make us perverts."

"Oh, Peg," she said, pushing past her, out of the

30

room, down the stairs and out of the house.

Peggy heard the car start up and take off with a squeal. What was going on? What was wrong with Jaret? She could just kill Claire! Quickly she dressed and went downstairs. Claire was waiting for her.

"Lovers' quarrel?"

"Yes," Peggy said. "Exactly. And it's your fault."

"I'm telling Daddy."

"Claire, I don't care who you tell. I love Jaret and I'm proud of it and the fact of the matter is you're just jealous because no one loves *you*. And if you tell Daddy, it's because you're consumed with envy." She gave Claire a push and was out the door.

When Peggy didn't see Jaret's car in front of her house she knew where she'd be. Washington Rock. It was up in the Grey Hills and they often went there to look at the view and talk.

As she drove up Huron Avenue she wondered why she'd said what she had to Claire. Everything was haywire today. She had in effect said that she and Jaret were . . . lovers. Why? Well, what if they were? She had a flash of lying in Jaret's arms and realized it made her happy, warm, content. Was that love? Sexual love? Would she want to kiss Jaret on the mouth?

"Who're you kidding?" she said aloud. Wasn't it amazing what secrets you could keep from yourself? Of course she would want to kiss her. And this was

31

not the first time she'd thought of it. Late at night, in her room alone, she'd held the pillow and pretended it was Jaret. Kissed the pillow. Just what kind of dumb game had she been playing anyway?

She turned into the parking lot. Only Jaret was here this early.

"Hi," she said, getting into Jaret's car.

Jaret looked straight ahead. "What are you doing here?"

"I came to see the view."

"Very funny."

"Jaret? Jaret, look at me."

"I can't."

"Why not?" Peggy wanted desperately to reach out and touch her, comfort her the way she'd been comforted.

"You wouldn't understand."

"You sound like me with my father."

She smiled. "Or me with mine, I guess. But you wouldn't understand, Peg. I just can't talk about it."

"About what?"

Jaret looked at her. "About what's bringing me down."

"Look, I know it's what Claire said. I know how it made you feel."

"That's just it, you don't," Jaret said. She picked some imaginary lint from her jeans.

"Okay, I don't. But I do."

32

They were silent for a few moments.

Then Peggy started to laugh. "I told Claire she was right. I said we were lovers."

"You what? Why?"

"I don't know," she answered, shrugging. "Something just came over me."

"Did you freak out or what?"

"I dunno."

"Well, for God's sake, Peg, what's going to happen?" Jaret gripped the steering wheel, knuckles turning whitish. "Claire will . . . well, she'll tell your father, won't she? I mean, that's what she said—you heard her. Oh, Peg, you must be crazy. She'll tell your father and then he'll lay it on mine and then no one will believe us and they won't let us see each other anymore. I can see it now. I'll be sent to my Aunt Sandy's in Texas. . . . Why did you do it? No one will believe us, Peg."

"Well, I guess we might as well be what they think, then, huh?" Peggy squeezed the edge of the vinyl seat, hands slippery with sweat.

Jaret stared at her. She understood what Peggy had said but she could think of no reply. Peggy must be kidding. But it wasn't funny to Jaret. She supposed she was expected to come back with some witty rejoinder, some smartass remark, some put-down of homosexuality. Well, she wasn't going to do that; she wasn't going to betray herself, not even for Peggy.

She looked away, through the windshield and out to the valley below. Everything was green, lush. It made her want to weep. Her eyes filled, vision blurred and slowly tears spilled over, ran down her cheeks. She couldn't move, did nothing to hide her tears.

"Jaret, why are you crying?" Now Peggy reached out, touched her shoulder, squeezed slightly, then moved closer, slipping her arm around Jaret. "Oh God, Jare, what is it? What did I say? I thought you . . . You see, I realized . . . Oh, Jare, I love you." There.

Jaret knew Peggy loved her as a sister, a friend. This repeated declaration only made the tears come faster, stronger.

"I don't understand, Jaret. Why are you crying? Don't you love me?"

Now she would have to answer she *did* love Peggy. Jaret nodded, tears still coming.

"Then why?"

If she didn't tell Peggy now Jaret knew their friendship would end. She couldn't live a lie. Peggy might as well know the truth and if she couldn't take it or was disgusted by it or hated Jaret for it, then it was better to know now for sure. Jaret wiped the tears from her face with her sleeve and turned to face Peggy, who looked bewildered, lost. Jaret smiled, taking in the generous mouth and slightly large nose.

"Oh, Peg," she finally said. "This is a mess. Damn Claire."

34

They were very near, faces closer than they'd ever been, except perhaps in the dark, in bed, when they whispered secrets. Jaret knew that with the slightest movement forward, head angled, she would be touching Peggy's lips with her own. Peggy knew this too. Almost imperceptibly, they each pulled back.

"Damn Claire," Peggy echoed, whispering. Her heart was thudding and she was both excited and frightened.

Jaret decided not another second could pass without her confession or she would die. "I don't think you understand, Peg. I don't think you know what's going on. Claire was right. I do love you that way. I have almost from the first day." Now that it was out she didn't disintegrate, feel slimy. She felt good. She began to breathe more regularly.

Peggy smiled. "Yes, I know. Me too. That's what I've been trying to tell you, you dumb gazinga."

Jaret didn't mean to say a stupid thing like: "What?" But she did. It was right out of a bad movie and they both laughed, breaking the terrible tension. When they stopped laughing and they returned to looking into each other's eyes, a different kind of tension began and finally ended as they naturally, sweetly kissed for the first time.

Claire hadn't told but always held it over their heads and never missed a chance to make a nasty comment.

"C'mon, Jare," Peggy said, "let's take that walk. The hell with Claire. She's just jealous. You know that."

"Yeah," said Jaret, not knowing that at all.

5

Claire sat on the edge of her bed, unable to stop trembling, inside and out. Rage always made her shake. She tried lighting a cigarette. It took four matches. She inhaled deeply, knowing, but not caring, that she was damaging her lungs. She could have killed them. They were disgusting. So smug, self-satisfied. So sure of themselves all the time. And what were they anyway? Queers. Dykes. Perverts. She'd learned in her psychology classes they were sexually immature, retarded. It was sick. And it made her want to vomit.

She stood up and walked across the room. There was no reason for the action and now that she was there she didn't know what to do. She walked to still another spot and found herself in front of the mirror. For years she had been telling herself to take the damn thing down. But she never did. Now she looked into it, hating what she saw. Everything was wrong. Her shoulders and hips were too wide, her breasts too small. She was short-waisted. And her face was a disaster. Her eyes were too close together, her nose too large, her mouth too full. If only she had been taller. It all might have worked on a larger person. But she was under five two. She spent half her time wishing she were different, an exercise in futility. She stubbed out her cigarette.

Why, she wondered for at least the four thousandth time, had Peggy gotten the looks? Even her slightly Roman nose gave her character, enhanced her. Why was life so unfair? Perhaps, Claire thought, she'd been a great beauty in another life and been cruel to someone ugly, laughed at a deformity, and now she was paying in this life. Claire was convinced she had lived many lives before, even though her belief was of little comfort in this life. This life was what she had to work with and it was hell. In this life she was a prisoner of her own body and her own face and there was no escaping either of them.

She lit another cigarette, sending up a smoke screen between herself and the mirror. Again her mind fixed on Peggy and Jaret. Both of them were attractive. Jaret might even be considered beautiful. Dammit, she *was* beautiful. If you liked the type, which Claire didn't. But by American standards, by *male* standards, she was a knockout. And that was what really made Claire crazy. Jaret Tyler could have had any boy or man she wanted and she wanted none. Peggy, too, could have had her pick. And who did they choose? Each other. It was sick. Crazy. Enraging. Why, when they could have the cream of the crop, did they want each other? She could have understood if they'd been ugly, as she felt she was, if they'd had no personalities, if they were dumb or something. Who'd want them then? But they had everything and still they persisted in this demented thing. It made Claire dizzy with frustration.

She lay down on her bed. The shaking had subsided and now, in its place, there was a dull pain in her stomach, the kind she had felt for weeks after her mother had died. Claire's mind went back to the day she'd discovered them in bed, to what Peggy had said to her: "I love Jaret and I'm proud of it and the fact of the matter is you're just jealous because no one loves you." And no one did. Not even her father, she felt. There was no one to love her. She'd never had a close friend and, of course, never a boyfriend. Her mother had always told her that she loved her but Claire had never believed it. Her mother had also told her she drove people away with her arrogance,

39

her air of superiority. Well, could she help being intelligent? What the hell else did she have besides that? Could she help it if it showed? Damn!

She jumped up, squashing the cigarette in the glass ashtray. Round and round never getting anywhere. She had not told her father about Jaret and Peggy for fear of what Peggy would say. Her father had eyes. Claire knew he could see how ugly she was. But as long as it remained unspoken, there was the slightest chance that it might not be true. If she told her father about Peggy and Jaret, Peggy could say: "She's making it up because she's jealous, because she can't get anyone to love her because she's so damn ugly." Claire sucked in her breath. Oh, no. Oh, no. If that was said out loud her father would have to acknowledge how horrid she was and then she would die. So she kept the secret, knowing she would never tell, but using it like a club whenever it suited her.

The thought of what Peggy might say to her father had propelled her back and forth across the room and, once again, she'd stopped in front of the mirror. Snatching up her hairbrush from the vanity, she threw it at the mirror, screaming, "I hate you, Peggy Danziger." But the mirror didn't shatter. Instead, the brush bounced off and hit Claire above her right eyebrow, breaking the skin. She stood there, her dreaded image staring back, a dribble of blood running down toward her eye. Typical, she thought, so damn typical.

6

June 25th

Summer vacation is only two days old and it's already
a drag. If only I had wheels. Mom was after me today
to do some stuff around the house like cleaning out
the cellar and attic. So why doesn't HE do it? All he
ever does when he's home is lie around and watch the
tube. So why should I have to work? I told her to
shove it and then she started crying and said she gets
no respect or anything so I felt sorry for her and told
her so and then I cleaned out the attic. Some fun.

Later me and some of the guys went down in the
woods to rap and hang out. Just when we were about

to leave we heard some sounds and we lay low. In a few secs we saw Jaret and Peggy come walking by real near us but they didn't see us. They were holding hands. Girls are really stupid. That Jaret is some chick but she acts like she thinks she's a movie star. Like she's above it all or something. Just 'cause she's good-looking doesn't give her the right to act that way it seems to me. Somebody ought to knock her around and put her in her place. She gives me a real pain. She thinks she's too good for all the guys around here. Chris says she writes to some guy at Yale and that's why she stopped going out with Gardener's Point guys. I'd like to do more than write to her. And maybe I will. Why not? Who the hell does she think she is anyway?

Tonight we hung out at the Bee Hive. This Jesus freak came in and we got in an argument with him and then I got him in a hammerlock and the jackass cried. I let him go and told him to stay outta the Hive. We won't see him again.

Tomorrow I promised to clean out the cellar for the Old Lady. Can't wait. Screw it.

7

Jaret's father was always tired when he came home from work. He owned a small but lucrative insurance firm. His office was in Riverbay, a half hour's drive away. Bert complained nightly that he was overworked and could never find efficient help. He hinted that life would be much better, easier, if only Kay would come to work for him. It was the last thing Kay Tyler was going to do. "Rather death," she'd said once when he asked her directly.

Kay wasn't against working, although she was very happy at home doing pottery and painting. She was against working for her husband. "The surest way to screw up a marriage is to spend twenty-four hours a day together," she said.

But that was exactly what Bert wanted. Twenty-*five*
hours a day would have been preferable, because he
was madly in love with his wife. She was, he insisted,
different, special, unique among women.

The main thing for Kay about Bert was his looks.
He often accused her of regarding him as nothing
more than a sex object and she had a hard time deny-
ing it. "Well, kid," she often said, "I can't help it if
you're a looker." "What about my mind?" he'd ask.
Kay would shrug and say, "Who needs it?"

Of course, she didn't really mean it. She just said
it to keep Bert aware of the way women were treated.
And he knew that. What he didn't know was that Kay
was not overwhelmed by his mind. She would have
preferred him to be a little more lively, quicker, with
interests beyond his business and *Time* magazine.
At twenty, when she had married him, she hadn't
known any better, hadn't seen beyond his looks. He'd
been five years older, with a kind of dashing air of
sophistication which she didn't find out until later
was nothing more than good taste in clothes and an
extraordinary sense of good food and wine. Not good
enough! But, oh, those looks.

It drove Kay mad that she was so shallow; such a
sucker for thick blue-black hair that grew in a perfect
widow's peak, huge, almost-black eyes, eyelashes
thicker and longer than any woman's she'd ever seen,

a nose meant for a sculptor's eye and a *real* mouth. Most men had stingy little mouths but not Bert. It was wide, beautifully shaped and lovely to kiss. And even though she'd been dead set against him growing it, the luxurious quality of his beard and mustache gave him an even more romantic look. He was short, only five feet seven, but Kay didn't mind as she was only five feet.

The truth of the matter was that Kay found *most* men dull. It was the rare man who could engage her. Bert thought he was an exception and Kay saw no point in correcting that impression. And, in a way, he was an exception; she loved him dearly. Aside from being gorgeous he was kind, considerate, gentle and loving. And that was a lot.

"Hello, darling," Bert said, handing Kay a small bouquet of sweetheart roses, something he did at least once a week. "How'd your day go?"

She sniffed the flowers, smiled, kissed his lovely mouth. "Thanks, honey. I made a really fantastic bowl. I'll show you after dinner."

"Great." He put an arm around her as they walked to the kitchen.

"How was your day?"

"Well, Helen botched up three letters and couldn't find Cohen in the file because she'd put it under *K*. I spent hours looking for the damn thing. My God, I'm tired."

"Seems to me if Cohen wasn't under *C* the most natural place in the world to look would be under *K*. Got to get on top of these things, kid!" She smiled at him, ruffled his hair.

"You see, that's exactly why I need you, Kay. Who else would think of that?"

"Don't," she warned. "Want a drink?"

He nodded.

The Tylers always had a cocktail hour before dinner and Jaret and Chris were welcome to join in the conversation, a prerogative Jaret sometimes exercised but one Chris never did anymore. When he was home he was invariably in the room he had built for himself in the basement.

This was one of the evenings Jaret had decided to sit with her parents, drinking the light vodka and tonic she was allowed since she turned eighteen. In the middle of their conversation, Chris, in satin soccer shorts and T-shirt, walked through the room.

"Want to join us, Chris?" Bert asked, always hopeful.

"Does a chicken have lips?" he answered, not bothering to look at anyone, continuing to walk toward the kitchen.

"God, I'm sick of that expression," Kay said. "Can't you come up with something new?"

He didn't answer. They heard him head downstairs to his room.

"I could strangle him," Kay said.

"Oh, Mom, he's just at that age."

"The age of a moron."

"Remember what I was like when I was sixteen?" Jaret asked as though it were twenty years ago rather than two.

"You bet. Articulate, bright, fun. Girls are always . . ." Kay stopped herself, realizing she shouldn't be a bigot about the male sex in front of Jaret. It wouldn't help things. "Actually, you were a pain in the neck."

"Right. We didn't get along at all then. Remember?"

Jaret, from age fourteen to sixteen, had been at terrible odds with her mother and it had scared and hurt Kay until she remembered how she'd been with her own mother and how they'd later become friends. That she and Jaret were good friends already was a real plus; she hadn't expected it for years.

"What a brat I was," Jaret went on.

"You were *never* a brat," Bert said. He was as entranced by his daughter as he was his wife. Jaret, aside from being exceptionally bright, had real beauty, and it pleased him to know that she would have her pick of men when the time came for her to marry.

"Of course I was, Daddy. You're always rewriting history."

He did it with everyone, everything. Bert liked to think of things as nice, pleasant, all the time. If some-

47

thing was upsetting and he was forced to see it, partici-
pate in it, as soon as it was over he blotted it out. If
it was referred to later he had dipped it in the honey
of his mind. He sighed. "I just don't remember you
being a brat."

"Oh, Bert," Kay said, "you're such a typical male."
Damn! She'd done it again. She glanced at Jaret to
see her reaction but her expression revealed nothing.

"I was a real drag," Jaret said. "So self-involved and
always thinking you and Mom were my enemies.
Don't you remember, Daddy? I called you the Head
Nazi!"

"Can't remember," Bert said a bit guiltily, knowing
they would both groan.

The expected sound came in unison.

A moment later the blast of music from the basement made them all start.

"Good God," Kay said, "I think he's put in another
speaker."

"What *is* it?" Bert asked.

"It's a new group," said Jaret. "The Awful Awfuls."

"When I was a kid Awful Awfuls were something
you drank."

Kay said, "Well now it's something you hear and it
is awful."

"I'll tell him to lower it," Bert said, rising.

When he left the room Kay tried to think of an

48

opening to amend the antimale things she'd said. Nothing clever or subtle came to her so she plunged right in. "Jare, what I said about your father being a typical male, well, I shouldn't have said it."

"Why not? Isn't he?"

What could she say to that? She didn't want to lie about what she really believed. She would just have to move around the question. "What I mean is, I sound like I'm putting men down all the time and I don't want to give that impression. You understand, kid?"

Jaret smiled. "Look, Mom, don't sweat it, because it doesn't matter what you say or don't say. I am the way I am."

"You're too damn smart, you know that?"

"I've been told that before."

"A real wiseacre," Kay said, laughing. But inside she felt down. A terrible guilt that she'd tried to ignore was growing daily and she didn't know what she was going to do about it.

Chris lay on his bed, staring at the *Star Wars* poster he'd glued to the ceiling. The Awful Awfuls were singing "Dirt in My Heart" and the black light gave the room the kind of mean glow Chris liked. He loved this room because it was his in every sense of the word. There had been no room before he'd built it. The space he occupied had simply been part of the basement.

"But you have a perfectly good room already," Kay said when he brought up the idea.

"I know, Mom, but it's on the same floor with everyone else."

"Well, pardon us for living, kid."

"Oh, come on. It's just that . . . a guy needs privacy." Would his mother think he was referring to masturbation? He blushed, even though he hadn't been.

"I've got news. *Everyone* needs privacy."

"Yeah, I know. Well, what difference does it make? I mean, why do you care?"

"I don't know. Somehow the thought of my son living in the cellar gives me the creeps. Like you're some kind of freak or something."

"Well, I *am* a freak," he said, grinning.

"Tell me. What will you build it out of?"

"Madras spreads."

He'd bought six of them, two per side, used one existing wall and now had a twelve-by-twelve room. The spreads were tacked to the ceiling and floor and, at two corners, attached to two-by-fours he had installed. A doorway cut in one spread operated like the flap of a tent. In the attic he'd found some pieces of old rugs that he'd sewn together, giving him wall-to-wall carpeting. He'd moved his mattress, desk and bookcase downstairs and in a junkyard he'd found an old dentist's chair which he'd painted purple. He'd built a platform for his mattress from pieces of wood he'd found in the basement. This was painted Chinese red. All in all, he and his friends agreed that the room was far out.

"Chris! Chris," Bert shouted.

"Yeah, Dad," he yelled over the music. "C'mon in."

Bert pushed through the flap. "Turn it down, Chris."

He jumped up, turned down the volume. "Was it loud?"

"Loud? You practically knocked us out of our chairs."

"Sorry, Dad. It didn't seem that loud to me."

Bert looked around the place Chris called his room and shook his head. "How can you see in here?"

"See?" Here we go again! The last time it was How can you breathe with no windows?

"Yes, see. It's pitch-black."

"It is?" It didn't seem black to Chris. To him it seemed cool.

"How can you study?" Bert tugged at his beard.

"Oh, I put that light on over by the desk when I'm studying." The truth was the light was there for show, for his parents. He always studied with the black light on.

"Good thing. You'd ruin your eyes otherwise."

51

Bert could have kicked himself. Couldn't he ever have a conversation with his son that wasn't nagging? Why couldn't he just talk to him? About what?

"Yeah, I know."

There was a moment of uncomfortable silence between them as the Awful Awfuls went on singing. Bert motioned toward the stereo. "Jaret said they're called the Awful Awfuls. When I was your age that was something I drank." He smiled, trying for contact.

Chris stared at his father, wondering what he was expected to say. "Oh, yeah?" was the best he could manage. He wished he could talk to him, maybe work out some of his problems. It would be neat if they could sit down and rap man to man like in books and movies but Chris just didn't know how to start. Even if he could think of an opening he couldn't imagine really rapping with his father. Whatever Chris said, he was sure his dad would put him down, criticize, lecture.

"Well," Bert said, touching the madras wall, "keep it down, will you, Chris?"

"Yeah, sure."

"See you at dinner."

"Right." Chris lay back down on the bed and turned toward the cellar wall, staring at his collection of photographs. He had taken them all. Some were sports photos; others were just pictures of people and nature. A few had been published in the local paper. Chris felt frightened in the pit of his stomach when he thought of the conversation he would have to have with his parents one day soon. He had no intention of going on to college. He hated school, saw no point to it. Not when what he wanted to be was a photographer. What difference would a college education make? All that junk about broadening yourself was for the birds. Nothing mattered to him except taking pictures. He already had a job promised the moment he could take it. Zach Summers had his own shop and portrait business and more work than he could handle. He was a neat guy and thought Chris's pictures were good. Zach was making plenty of money and *he* hadn't gone to college.

Still, the thought of telling his parents made Chris feel weak-kneed. Not that they were *so* awful. His mom, especially, was a pretty good listener. But they were both really hot on education and he couldn't imagine that they'd understand his wishes. Well, at least he didn't have to talk about it tonight.

He rolled over on his bed, now facing the madras wall with the posters from *Charlie's Angels, Welcome Back, Kotter* and *Happy Days*. He didn't really know why he'd put up posters from TV shows except he needed something and that's what most of the guys had. He'd never in his life seen any girls who looked like Charlie's Angels and he wasn't sure he wanted to.

There was something about them that was kind of scary, unreal. The best-looking girls he'd ever seen were in his class: Sarah Kartalia and the Crawford sisters, Amy and Annie. And, though he'd never tell her, Jaret. Thinking of her made him remember the lie he'd told the guys.

Chris was not usually a liar. In fact, he hated lying, knowing it always got you in trouble. And he despised most the kind of lies the guys told about girls. Since they probably all knew they were all lying, he wondered why they kept doing it. Mid Summers was the worst. It amazed Chris that two brothers could be so different. Mid was as loud as Zach was quiet, as rough as Zach was gentle. Mid was always bragging about some girl or other that he'd made it with but Chris didn't believe him. Not that he wasn't good-looking; but something about his boasts just didn't ring true. Chris really didn't like Mid much but the other guys seemed to so he said nothing. It was Mid who had caused him to lie about Jaret.

They'd been sitting in the woods rapping, Mid, Roger, Stephen, Jake and him, when they heard the sound of people walking. They hit the dirt and peered through the bushes. It was Jaret and Peggy. They were holding hands and walking very close together. After they went by Mid said, "What are they, queers?"

All the guys laughed.

It made Chris feel sick. "Yeah, sure," he said

bravely. "They're just mad for each other."

Then there were some remarks about how good Peggy's body was and some about Jaret, slightly less gross because of Chris's presence. But Mid wouldn't let it go.

"So how come Jaret never goes out with anyone?"

"What makes you think she doesn't?" Chris asked, feeling defensive.

"I know what goes on in this town, buddy-boy. She hasn't had a date in months. What happened to her and Pete Cross?"

"He's a turkey." Chris knew this was ridiculous. Pete Cross was captain of the football team and everyone knew he was not a turkey. "Cross was too young for Jaret. She's making the scene with this dude from Yale."

"Oh, yeah? What's his name?"

"What's the difference?" Chris was stalling for time and a name.

"Where'd she meet him?" Roger asked.

Chris felt panicky, unused to making up stories and unsure why he was doing it. "They met at Christmas, at a party of my cousin's."

"What's his name?" Mid asked again.

"John Williams. What's it to you?"

Mid shrugged. "Just wondered."

"He writes her at least three times a week. He's cool."

That had been the end of it and Chris had tried not

to think of it again, reluctant to examine his reasons for inventing John Williams. But now the time had come.

When Jaret broke up with Pete, Chris didn't give it much thought; he never gave much thought to his sister's life. But now he had to wonder. Why *would* she break up with the best guy in the senior class? Pete was good-looking and smart, and all the girls were after him. Of course, Chris didn't really know him and maybe Cross *was* a turkey. Jaret was pretty smart and it would take a really smart guy to satisfy her. Or maybe no guy. Maybe it *was* Peggy.

The thought made Chris feel strange, uncomfortable. He didn't understand what he was thinking. All he really knew was that Jaret had changed since she and Peggy Danziger became best friends. She seemed happier, for one thing. And something was different about the way Jaret treated Peggy. He couldn't put his finger on it but it was not the same way she treated Bianca. When Mid had said maybe Jaret and Peggy were queer it had hit home somehow.

Chris began to sweat. The thought of Jaret and Peggy together . . . well, he just couldn't understand it. What would they do? He could picture them kissing, although it seemed stupid, but that was as far as he could go. He hadn't had that trouble when Jaret was going out with Pete Cross. He'd often had fantasies about his sister and Pete and been ashamed of

56

them until Roger told him he'd imagined his sister with her boyfriend. Chris decided then that all brothers must do that and that it was perfectly all right. But did all brothers think about their sisters with other girls? Does a chicken have lips?

The whole thing was too confusing. If Jaret was a queer he didn't want to know about it. As far as he was concerned, she was going with John Williams from Yale and that was that.

8

July 2nd

The Creep came for his weekly meal tonight. Some Big Deal he thinks he is. And She practically falls all over him like he's doing her some big favor by coming over to eat. It makes me want to puke. It's the one time I feel sorry for Himself. She acts like the Creep's her husband instead of her son and Himself is just left right out. Poor turkey.

Hung out at the Bee Hive. Nothing much doing. That yo-yo Joe Carter came tooling down in his Maverick and asked me and the guys if we wanted to go for a ride, so we did even though he's a jerk. What the hell, wheels are wheels. We rode around town and checked out the spots. Nothing. Took a drive up to Washington Rock and scared the pants off some of the kids making out in their cars by flashing a light on them. They thought we were the pigs.

Back to the B.H. No action. Got home at ten thirty. Watched a dumb movie. There was this chick in it, Donna something, and she really pissed me off the way she went boogying around that flick. Just like Jaret. She needs somebody to knock her on her ass. Who do these chicks think they are, anyway? I'd show her what's what if I had the chance. Dumb broad.

9

The Fourth of July was a perfect summer day. Warm, but low humidity; not a cloud in the sky. The traditional Fourth in Gardener's Point began at nine in the morning at the polo grounds near the high school with various competitions. There were three-legged races, sack races, relay races. Fifty-yard dashes and a bicycle race. People of all ages entered and the whole thing ended around eleven thirty with a tug of war. Children under fourteen usually decorated their bicycles with red, white and blue crepe paper. There was a conspicuous absence of competitors between the ages of fifteen and twenty-one, an age group which considered the competitions much too childish. However, if these same young people returned to Gardener's Point after college graduation, or if they simply turned twenty-one, they had a new perspective and competing was all right again.

In the afternoon there was a circus in Wilson Park; at night the fireworks were displayed there. The bleachers that had been set up for the circus remained, but most people brought blankets and lay on the ground to watch the display.

The year before Jaret had gone to the fireworks with Pete Cross and Peggy had gone with her boyfriend of the summer, Eric Kramer. This year when Peggy and Jaret told Bianca they were planning to go together, alone, Bianca was horrified.

"You can't mean it," she said, putting a hand to each temple. "You sim-ply cannot."

"Why not?" Peggy asked.

"It is ab-so-lute-ly the worst thing I have ever heard!" She puffed loudly on her cigarette.

"You mean," Jaret said, winking at Peggy while Bianca's eyes were shut, "that you have *never* heard a worse thing?"

"What?" Streams of smoke poured from Bianca's mouth.

"I think," Peggy said, "Jaret is accusing you of hyperbole. Excess."

"Excess. Yes, of course. One *must* be excessive with you two. If you go to the pyrotechnic display . . ."

"Pyrotechnic display?" said both Jaret and Peggy.

"Ah, what peasants you are. Why do I put up with you?" Bianca tried, but failed, to drape her body over the back of the couch. Her hips just wouldn't move the way she desired.

"You put up with us because you love us," Jaret said. "And we love you."

"If that is true then I implore you, do not go to the pyro- . . . fireworks alone." Bianca stubbed out one cigarette and immediately planted a new one in her holder.

Jaret said, "You know, you're off the wall with those cigarettes."

"It's stress and *you* are causing it."

"I don't know where she's coming from, do you?" Jaret asked Peggy.

Peggy shook her head, started braiding her hair.

"I am trying to tell you ri-dic-u-lous people that no one, *no one,* goes to the display"—she smiled quickly—"without dates, unless they are in a crowd."

"Whose gazinga is that?" Peggy asked.

"It is an unwritten rule but *it is there*," Bianca said, as though announcing the end of the world. In a stage whisper she added: "Only creeps go in twos without dates."

"Well," Jaret said, "I guess we're creeps."

"I think I'm going to have a stroke." Bianca put her hand over her heart. "You should feel my heart, just feel it pounding."

62

"Strokes are not caused by pounding hearts," Peggy said. "Heart attacks rely on the heart for trouble. Strokes come from the brain."

"The point is you are driving me in-sane. Do you have any idea of what I go through?" She was lying on the couch now, one arm across her brow.

"What?" Jaret asked, munching on a chocolate chip cookie Peggy had made. "Tell."

"Well," she said, warming to the subject, "for instance, Mary Lou and Betsy. You've sim-ply dropped them, you know, Peggy. Not nice. Not nice at all. They keep asking me what you are up to. *Well*, what can I say?"

"What *do* you say?" asked Peggy.

"I say that you are involved in a very important, secret project with Jaret."

"Oh, wow! Come on. Important, secret project! Wow!"

"Well, what *can* I say? They are driving me in-sane with their incessant questions. And Nancy Aucrbacher, too. Not that she asks *me* anything, of course." She shook her head, the frizz bobbing frantically.

"What about Nancy?" Jaret asked.

"Well, she says you're a square. She says you dropped out of their crowd after they tried to get you to rip off some stuff with them from Baron's Drugs. I mean, after all, Jaret, you don't want them thinking that, do you?"

Jaret smiled. "As a matter of fact, I don't mind them thinking that at all because it's the truth. My meeting Peggy and that incident kind of coincided. They just didn't get it, you know? I mean, wow. How could a potential lawyer get involved in ripping off a store? I tried to explain but no comprende. Besides, I don't think it's cool . . . or right. So I'm a square."

"Honest, sí, square, no," Peggy said.

"Sí, no, no, sí . . . this is getting us nowhere," Bianca said.

"Where do we want to get?"

"I'm trying to impress upon you that people are talking. I mean, two of the best-looking females in the senior class and all of a sudden you stop going out with guys and you're seen everywhere together. What do you think people are saying?"

"What?"

"Well, they think . . . Well, they don't know exactly. . . . They just think you're strange. Of course, the *truth* is the last thing that occurs to them, naturally."

"Why naturally?"

"Oh, Jaret, no one thinks of *that*." The whole situation was growing more impossible for Bianca. She dearly loved her two friends and she tried desperately to understand what it was they felt for each other. But try as she might she simply couldn't comprehend how they could prefer each other to males.

She didn't put them down but she worried about them, their reputations, their futures, and she just didn't get it.

"Look, Bianca," Jaret said, "I know it's hard for you and you've been very loyal to us but I just don't see how going to the fireworks alone will jeopardize our lives in any way."

"Will you be sitting in the bleachers or lying on a blanket?"

Peggy said, "Lying on a blanket."

"Oh, my God! Who plans your act, Evel Knievel?" Despairing, she fell once again into the couch cushions.

Peggy and Jaret looked at each other. What could they do to calm their friend? They were used to Bianca's overdramatizations; it was part of *her* act, part, they supposed, of being an actress. But, exaggerated or not, they knew she was genuinely concerned for them.

"What do you want us to do, stay home?"

"I think you should go with me and Zach and lie on our blanket. No, there wouldn't be enough room. Put your blanket right next to ours and we'll all sort of lie around together like the ancient Romans." She grinned, trying to show how much fun it would be.

"Won't that sort of cramp your style?" Peggy asked.

"Just *what* do you think Zach and I would be doing in public? Really!"

"Well, what do you think Peggy and I would be doing?"

"It's different. I don't want people thinking my two best friends are . . ."

"Are what?" Jaret asked, a touch of anger in her voice.

"Oh, not *that*. . . . I told you, no one thinks of *that*."

"I wish," Peggy said, "you'd stop saying *that* that way."

"Sorry, my darlings. I don't mean to offend." It was her best Katharine Hepburn voice. "I simply wish to protect. I do not wish my two best friends thought of as . . . loners."

"Oh, Bianca," Jaret said.

"We don't care," said Peggy.

"I care." Bianca tried to imagine Zach leaving her and within seconds the tears filled her eyes. "Don't you have any regard for me?"

To avoid the full scene Peggy jumped in. "All right, all right. We'll go with you and Zach. Okay, Jare?"

"Neat."

"You're good women." Bianca dabbed at her eyes. "I shan't forget this."

When Bianca told Zach he wasn't exactly thrilled.

"Are you saying you don't care for my friends?" Bianca used her haughtiest voice although ordinarily she minimized her affectations around him.

66

"Honey, c'mon. I like them, I really do. It's just that I wanted to be alone with you. Besides, how come they don't have dates? I know at least five guys who'd like to go out with them. Want me to fix them up?"

"NO," she said, much too quickly. "I mean, they . . . well, they're into Women's Liberation and they're trying to get along without men. It's an experiment." What a perfect explanation, she thought. Why hadn't it occurred to her before? That would be her standard line from now on when anyone asked.

"Well, *I'm* a man. How come they want to share *my* blanket?"

"You're not their date. Oh, please, Zachariah, let's not go on and on about it. We'll be alone afterward. I mean, they won't go out with us or anything."

"Okay, honey, if that's what you want."

Zach Summers was absolutely crazy about Bianca and willing to do almost anything for her. There had been a number of other girls in his life but Bianca was different. She was going to college and then to New York to try to be an actress and, at twenty-two, Zach was not naive enough to think that she'd remain faithful to him. But he tried to remain philosophical about it.

"Oh, thanks, love."

Bianca kissed him gently, pulled away and looked deep into his gray eyes. They were not only beautiful

67

but kind. When she'd met Zach, six months before, she had just about given up on the male population of Gardener's Point. They were, in her opinion, either dudes or duds. She had decided she would live the life of a nun until college. Surely the men in Chicago would be an improvement. But then she met Zach. Of course, she'd seen him around town for years and been in his shop many times. But when she went in that day in January to pick up some pictures for her mother, they looked at each other as though they'd never seen each other before.

And when they went out that first time, three days later, she realized that one of the reasons the boys in Gardener's Point held no appeal for her was because they were exactly that: boys. Zach was a man. And what a man. He wasn't trying to prove anything or to show off. He was never macho. He was interested in what she had to *say*. And he was kind, thoughtful, gentle. Most of all, he respected her desire to be an actress and never made fun of her. And last, but not least, he was six feet five!

It had crossed Bianca's mind to skip college and acting and to marry Zach. She hinted at it once.

"Bianca," he said, "I think you're proposing to me."

"You're very smart."

"You're very obvious."

"Well?" she asked.

"I'm going to turn you down. Let me tell you why.

68

It would be real easy to say yeah, let's get married as soon as you graduate from high school. But I'm not going to do that even though I love you and would dig it. I mean, in a way I would."

"But you won't want to be tied down," she said, supplying his reason, protecting herself.

"Try to listen, honey. It's because I love you that I'm not going to do it. See, if you married me this summer you'd probably move into my apartment and then maybe you'd get a job. Now what would that job be?"

"There's not much to do around here."

"You got it. Anyway, no matter what you did, for a while we'd be real happy, you know, being in love and everything. But eventually . . . Well, let me skip to ten years from now. You'd be twenty-eight and we'd probably have two or three kids and whenever you'd look at television or go to the movies you'd sit there all angry, thinking: 'I could do better than that. If only I'd had the chance.' And then you'd hate and resent me and hate the kids and probably we'd end up divorced and bitter and . . ."

"All right, all right," she said. "I get your point."

"If you want, we'll talk about it again in five or six years."

And they both knew that they probably wouldn't.

"But for now," he said, "let's enjoy what we've got, okay?"

She had agreed. Now they never mentioned the

future but tried to enjoy every moment they had together as much as possible.

The two couples laid their blankets side by side,
settling themselves. Bianca had told her friends the
Women's Liberation story she'd given Zach and,
though they thought it ridiculous, they agreed to go
along if he brought it up.

"It's nice of you to let us join you, Zach," Peggy
said.

"My pleasure. Listen, I know some very nice
guys . . . I mean, unusual guys and . . ."

"No thanks, Zach," Jaret said kindly.

"How long will your experiment last?"

"As long as we're happy," Peggy answered. It was
something they had said to each other many times.
They would be together as long as it made them both
happy.

"And this boycott of males is making you happy?"
He wasn't baiting them; he really wanted to know.

"For now," Peggy said.

Jaret looked at her, feeling a pang of insecurity,
but Peggy managed, in the dark, to press Jaret's hand
with her own, indicating the remark was for Zach's
benefit.

"There goes your brother, Zach, and yours, Jaret,"
Bianca said.

Mid, Chris and some of their friends, still young

70

enough to be acceptable without dates, were crossing the park, carrying blankets.

Zach frowned. "I worry about him. He seems sort of screwed up, unhappy, you know? Is your brother like that?"

"I don't know. He never talks to me. I think they're all off the wall at that age," Jaret said.

"I guess. It's hard to remember."

The first burst of fireworks was shot off with a whizzing sound; red streaks, blue, then little gold curlicues and a final bang. Everyone oohed and clapped.

They lay on their backs, Bianca resting her head on Zach's shoulder, his arm around her. Peggy and Jaret were side by side, only their pinkies touching, each feeling a private resentment.

10

Being alone, to touch, to love, had become very difficult for Peggy and Jaret. Because of Claire's attitude Jaret felt too uncomfortable to stay overnight at Peggy's, and Jaret's mother's knowing made them both uneasy. But now that the weather was warm life had become somewhat easier. They'd discovered a secluded spot deep in the woods, a small clearing guarded by tall pines in a circle. It was as though it had been made especially for them.

After the fireworks they drove there, parking the car where no one would see it, walking the half mile to their spot. They spread out their blanket and lay down on it. The moon sent slivers of light through the trees, making it possible for them to see one another dimly. They faced each other, eyes looking deep into eyes. Their lips touched lightly; arms and legs intertwined as their kiss became stronger and their bodies pressed closer. When their lips parted each burrowed into the other's neck, ear.

"I love you so," Peggy said.

"Oh, Peg, me too; you."

They pulled back, bodies still close but their faces an inch or so apart so they could see each other.

"It really drove me up the wall tonight," Jaret said.

"What did, Cree Cree?" Peggy stroked Jaret's hair.

"All the other couples lying there wound up in each other and all we could do was link pinkies like two five-year-olds."

"I know. It was a humungus feeling. Makes me not want to go places, know what I mean?" Peggy said.

"Course I do. It's the pits. But it'll be different when we're in college."

"Will it? We'll still be sneaking around, Jare. How will it be different?"

"It won't feel like sneaking. I mean, meeting each other in Boston and stuff. How's that sneaking? And then after we graduate we'll go to New York and you'll get a job in publishing and I'll go to Columbia Law and we'll live together and . . ."

"Jare, don't."

"Why not? Isn't that what you want too?" Jaret felt Peggy stiffen slightly. Why did she always have to question everything? Couldn't she, for once, let things alone?

"Sure, it's what I want," Peggy said uneasily, "but it's a long way off, babe. I mean, who knows what might happen between now and then?"

Too quickly, Jaret said, "Like what?"

"Relax. I don't know. But anything could happen. I could die, for instance."

Jaret covered Peggy's mouth with her hand. "Don't say that. Don't ever say that."

Peggy took her hand away. "Well, it's true, Jaret. You can't plan anything in this life. There *are* no happy endings, you know."

"What's that supposed to mean?"

"It means even if two people really dig each other and stay faithful and all that gazinga for fifty years or more, one of them is probably going to die before the other and that's hardly a happy ending."

"You're really bringing me down," Jaret said, rolling over on her back, staring at the stars through the opening in their leafy ceiling.

"I'm sorry. But it's like I said from the beginning, you know—as long as we're happy. There's no percentage in planning. Look at my mother and father."

"That's why you're so morbid and creepy about all this, isn't it? You think because it happened to them it's gonna happen to you, me, everyone."

74

Peggy went on as though she hadn't heard. "You should've seen their plans. Like for the next fifty-five years. And they were always rapping about the future and putting everything off. . . . Do you know that they hadn't taken a vacation in ten years because they were saving everything for this year they were gonna have in Europe. Humungus!"

"It doesn't mean that's going to happen to us. Them, sí, us, no."

Peggy looked at her. "You don't understand," she said quietly.

"So explain."

"It's simple. All we have is *now* . . . really. Think about it. So we have to concentrate on now. Except for school and meeting each other for weekends and stuff, well, there's no point in making long-range plans. We could change too."

Jaret felt sick. "You mean, like not love each other anymore?"

Peggy took Jaret's hand, stroked the back of it. "It could happen."

"I'll never stop loving you."

"You don't really know that, Jare."

"I do. It's you, isn't it? You're thinking about yourself. It's *you* who might stop loving *me*. Isn't that what you're saying? Huh?"

"It could happen to either. I don't know. It sure doesn't seem that way now but who knows? Anything could happen."

"Oh, stop saying that." Jaret pulled away, turning her back.

"Jaret? Come on. Don't spoil this night. Jare? Cree Cree? I'll have to get Sparky over here to see what's wrong, I guess. Sparky, c'mere," she called out, "Char wants you to see what's wrong with Cree Cree."

Jaret started to laugh and Peggy could feel it.

"Come on, Cree Cree. Sparky and Char want to play." She began to tickle Jaret, who rolled over, protecting herself. "Ah, there's Cree Cree."

"You nut," Jaret said, laughing.

"Me nut, you not!"

"Come here." Jaret put her arms around Peggy and held her close. "I love you, Char."

"As long as we're happy, Jaret?" Peggy asked.

"As long as we're happy," Jaret answered, and kissed Peggy's eyes, cheeks, mouth.

Kay was still up, reading in the living room, when Jaret came in. "Hi, toots. Have a good time?"

"Sure." Jaret felt odd about the question and reply.

"Good fireworks?" Kay marked the place in her book and set it on the table near her. She lit a cigarette.

"Pretty good. They seem dimmer and shorter every year though." She didn't want a conversation. She wanted to go to bed and think of Peggy.

"That's because you're getting older. What'd you do after?"

Jaret shifted her weight from one foot to the other. "Mom, *please.*"

For a second Kay didn't understand, felt hurt. Then the meaning of her daughter's plea dawned on her. She swallowed, pressed her lips together. "Sorry." She looked away, not knowing what to say next. Where did you go from there?

Jaret ended her quandary. "Well, I'm going up. Good night, Mom."

Kay forced a smile. "Good night, kid." She picked up her book, opened it, stared at the page. When she heard Jaret hit the top stair she closed the book and slowly lowered it to her lap.

The days of Jaret coming in from an evening out, talking and laughing about it, were over. It made Kay feel old, lonely. She missed Jaret terribly. And of course Chris was no consolation; he shared nothing. Besides, it was different with a mother and son. But a mother and daughter had a kind of closeness that no other two people had. Or at least they could. She'd once had it with Jaret, and she knew, if patient, she'd have it again. But for now the nature of Jaret's relationship had put a small wedge between them.

And what if that relationship had been with a boy? Would Jaret be so secretive, so protective of her privacy? Of course. Kay remembered a relationship of her own at the same age. Had she shared her love feelings for George Blake with her mother? Not on your life! Because, instinctively, she knew there was no way her mother would, could, understand. After all, what did her mother know of true love? Kay smiled. Surely Jaret's feelings were similar. Kay's smile faded. What was the use of this kind of thinking? This was different. Wasn't it?

She walked to the kitchen, opened the fridge and took out a quart of milk. She poured herself a glass, put away the container and stood at the sink, staring out at the night as she drank. There was nothing to see but her own reflection. What was it that bothered her the most? That her daughter was having an affair with another girl or, simply, that she was having a *sexual* affair? Kay was sure Jaret and Peggy were beyond the hand-holding stage. After all, Jaret was eighteen. Surely the relationship was of a sexual nature. And if Peggy had been a boy? Wouldn't it be sexual then? How would she feel about that? It was so damn confusing.

A dragging, shuffling noise interrupted her thoughts. It was Chris, coming up from the basement. He stood for a moment just inside the kitchen door, his long, dark hair tangled from bed, two strands sticking straight up like enormous horns. His tall, thin body was draped in a sheet as he stared at her, blinking, blue eyes, like his mother's, adjusting to the light.

"My God," Kay said, "it's like some awful mole coming up for air."

"Nmghph," he grunted.

"Is that right?" This was the second time she'd seen him that night, and the total of what he'd said to her so far was "Nghft" and "Nmghph." "What can I do ya, kid?"

"Thirst," he mumbled.

With her thumb she gestured toward the refrigerator.

Chris shuffled across the tiled floor, his sheet trailing behind him like a long tail.

"I don't need the floor cleaned," Kay said. "Don't you wear pajamas anymore?"

Head in the refrigerator, he said, "Does a chicken have lips?"

Kay screamed. "I cannot stand it. Please, please, I beg of you, find a new expression."

When he turned around with a root beer in his hand he was amazed to see his mother on her knees in a praying position.

"Far out," he said.

"Better, but not good enough! Honestly, Chris," she said, rising, "it really is a bore, you know."

He popped open his can of soda and said, "Ghmpnh."

"Swell, thanks."

Hiking up his sheet, he headed for the door to the basement.

"Good night, Chris. Thanks for the intelligent, stimulating conversation."

He shuffled along silently.

"Can't you even say good night?"

Without turning, he said, "Does a snake have ears?" And he was gone.

Kay had to laugh. At least the kid still had a sense of humor, even if he was the most inarticulate boob of all time. Well, it would pass . . . wouldn't it? Of course. She washed out her glass, stuck it in the drainer and went back to her chair in the living room.

She lit a fresh cigarette. Kay had read everything she could find on the subject of homosexuality and lesbianism and what she'd read wasn't that helpful. There were many theories as to why a person turned out to be a lesbian—environment, chromosomes, choice—and a lot of big, fat blanks. No one really seemed to know. Nevertheless, Kay couldn't help blaming herself and Bert. But why *blame*? Why the need to put it in those terms? She knew it was because she still had one foot in the fifties and a lesbian life-style was not what she'd had in mind for her daughter; it was not something Kay could fully accept as normal, no matter how liberated she might be.

Oh, what a fraud she was! Pretending to Jaret it was all fine with her, simply swell, because she wanted Jaret to *like* her, to think she was cool! What she really wanted to do was throw herself at Jaret's feet and beg her to see a psychiatrist so she'd get over this thing. Kay didn't think it was dirty or disgusting or bad; but she did think it was a way of life that could only make Jaret unhappy, even though it was more acceptable now than when she'd been Jaret's age.

What were their names? Olive something and Claire or Clara, yes, Clara Wilson and Olive . . . Olive . . . oh, what the hell. They'd been freshmen in college and Clara and Olive were discovered in bed together. What a scene! Girls screamed when they heard; some said it actually made them vomit. And what had *she* done? She'd been no better. She and her best friend had written and acted in a skit portraying Olive and Clara "In Love." Ah, yes, it brought down the house.

Kay felt flushed with shame thinking of this now. She'd heard later that Clara Wilson killed herself. No one knew what had happened to Olive. Did lesbians kill themselves anymore? Did she fear that Jaret would suffer humiliation, tortures she couldn't take? Was it simply a mother's protective instinct? Or was it something else? Something like being reactionary, embarrassed, guilty? Was she, in the end, simply and hopelessly square?

And she hadn't even told Bert. She'd conned herself, saying he had enough on his mind, leaving her alone with this problem which she deeply resented. Yet it was her own decision. Perhaps she *should* tell Bert after all. But could he accept his daughter's sexuality, especially when it involved lesbianism? Oh, why bother him? She was strong enough to carry this knowledge alone for a little longer. And then Jaret would be gone and perhaps there would be no need to deal with it, for a while anyway. Cowardly? Yes. Sensible? Yes. Settled? Yes. Good. Perfect.

Then why did she feel so awful?

II

July 4th

The fireworks were a big drag. In the crowd, I got
separated from the guys. Bumped into Joe Carter. He
was gonna drive me down to the Bee Hive and then
as we were getting in the car I saw Jaret and Peggy
getting into Peggy's car. I had this idea. I told Carter
to follow them—he'd do anything you tell him. . . .
I think he pretended he was a secret agent or some
dumb thing. What a turkey. So anyway we followed
them. About two blocks away from it I could tell they
were going to the woods so I told Carter to pull over.
We got out and went the rest of the way by foot and

just as we got near the woods I saw her taillights turn down Apple Path. We kept following. . . . My old Boy Scout training came in handy. . . . We were real quiet. They parked the car and got out. I couldn't figure what they were gonna do but I knew I wasn't gonna miss it—no way. They started walking deeper into the woods. Me and Carter kept far enough behind but didn't lose sight of them. The moon was full so we could see pretty good. . . . Anyway they had on a flashlight so it was easy to follow that.

Once Carter stepped on a twig that cracked and the girls stopped and looked around, then they went on. When they started walking again I gave Carter a really hard look and then pinched him like murder. At the same time I put my hand over his mouth so he couldn't scream or anything. I didn't have to say a word. He knew what I meant and what I'd do if he made any more noise. What a look he had in his eyes when I squeezed his fat skin. Far out. So we kept following them. Then they went into this kind of cleared place which I'd never noticed before. Me and Carter snuck up as close as we could get behind some big trees and weeds. The moonlight was coming through the trees real good. The chicks put a blanket on the ground and lay down. And then I almost choked. They lay real close, facing each other, and then they kissed and got all tangled up. I looked at Carter and he looked at me. I thought he might pass out right then and there. I could tell he wanted to laugh but I gave him a look that said I'd waste him on the spot if he did. He looked away.

Well, then they started talking real soft so we couldn't hear. Then it seemed like maybe they were hassling about something. Next Peggy yelled out "Sparky" and "Creaker" or some dumb thing. After a while Peggy put her hand inside Jaret's blouse and before I knew it, before I could believe it, they were doing IT to each other. That's right, IT. And they really acted like they dug it. I could hardly believe it—Jaret Tyler and Peggy Danziger . . . two queers! Goddamn far out.

Well, we watched until they finished and then we got the hell out of there. I told Carter not to tell anybody, told him I'd rip out his eyes if he did. There'll be time to tell . . . when it's right.

So I made up my mind tonight. It won't be easy but I'll find a way. That's what brains are for. I'll plan it real careful and before the summer's over I'll do it. Nothing can stop me now. I'm gonna get Jaret Tyler.

12

Usually at dinner time Tom Danziger had a patient or was at the hospital or Peggy was at Jaret's or she and Jaret had a burger out. Claire was always at home. But this was the first night in a very long time that all three had had a meal together. Dr. Danziger barely noticed. He just happened to be there. Claire, knowing in advance that he was to be home, had prepared veal piccata, fresh string beans, an avocado salad and lemon mousse for dessert. She watched as he took his first bite of veal. He said nothing, staring into space.

Peggy watched Claire watching her father. "This is neat, Claire," she said.

"Thanks," Claire mumbled, not looking at her.

They waited again as he took another bite. Nothing.

"Daddy," Peggy said, "isn't this veal super?"

"Hmmm?"

"The veal. Isn't it delicious?"

"Oh, yes, yes, very good," he said absently.

Peggy tried to kick him under the table but she couldn't reach. "The string beans are so fresh," she went on, sounding like a commercial.

"Fresh," Tom repeated, nodding like a puppet.

Seeing Claire's saddened face, Peggy ached for her sister. As much as she loved her father she was growing impatient with his apathy, his grief, if that's what it was. "Oh, Daddy," she said, "can't you pay a little bit of attention? Claire went to all this trouble and . . ."

"Shut up," Claire said.

Peggy was shocked and looked at Claire with surprise.

"Just shut up," Claire hissed through clenched teeth.

Tom put down his fork and actually looked at his two daughters. "What's going on?"

"Nothing, Daddy. Never mind. It's nothing. Just eat your dinner." Claire talked to him as though he were a child.

Tom squinted through his glasses, cocked his head slightly to one side. "Don't talk to me that way, Claire," he said gently.

"What way, Daddy?"

"Like . . . like . . ." He waved a hand as though he were too tired to continue.

"Like he's a child," Peggy supplied.

"Shut up," Claire said again.

"Oh, Claire, I'm just trying to help."

"Well, don't. I don't need help from a person of your ilk."

"Now *you* shut up," Peggy spat at her after glancing at her father.

Tom Danziger leaned on his elbow and pleated his lower lip with thumb and forefinger as he looked at his two daughters with bewilderment.

"Just keep it up," Claire said, "and you know what'll happen."

"Shove it," Peggy snapped.

"Hey, hey," Tom finally said. "What is this? What are you two fighting about?"

Claire turned toward her father, pasted a smile on her face. "I'm sorry, Daddy. It's really nothing." She turned toward Peggy, same smile, but a warning in her eyes. "We shouldn't be doing this at mealtime, dear. You know what Daddy's always taught us about digestion."

Peggy felt like smacking her and looked away, disgusted.

"The hell with the digestion," Tom said. "I want to know what's going on. What's this stuff about *person of your ilk*, for instance?"

Peggy held her breath involuntarily.

"Just an expression, Daddy," Claire said.

"Why is it I don't believe you, Claire?"

Peggy breathed.

This was not going the way Claire'd planned it. Why was it that whenever she imagined something it turned out so different? If she didn't get the conversation onto something else quickly she was afraid she might cry. "I was wondering, Daddy, will you be hiring a housekeeper this fall?"

"A housekeeper? No. Why?"

Claire felt relieved, knowing she had successfully diverted him. "Well, we'll both be gone. Who will take care of you?"

"*I* will," he said flatly. "Housekeepers are for men a bit older, I think." He cleared his throat, took a sip of wine, cleared his throat again. "Actually," he said, trying for a smile, a kind of casual laugh, "I'll probably get married."

His daughters froze as though caught in a stop-action film shot. Peggy's fork was in her mouth, Claire's halfway there. Tom, unable to bear their reactions, looked away, continued eating.

Peggy removed her fork from her mouth and laid it down on the plate like something loathed. Claire followed suit.

It had only been seven months since Erica had died. He'd seemed so bereaved. How could he be talking about remarrying? Peggy couldn't believe he'd actually said it. "Get married?" she said, parrot-like.

"I . . . well, you know," he said, not looking up from his plate.

"No," Claire said, "I don't know." Her tone was harsh, punishing.

Tom snapped his head up. He made a cleft in his chin with his fingers. "I'm forty-three years old," he said.

"So you have plenty of time," Claire answered.

"Yes, sure. I just want you to realize that, well, I'm not going to stay a bachelor forever."

"You're not a *bachelor*," Claire said officiously. "You're a widower."

A kind of guilt overrode his desire to comment on his daughter's tone. "I know what I am, Claire," he said sadly.

"Oh, Daddy." Peggy reached out to touch him. He looked at her, then covered her hand with his large one.

Claire absorbed the scene, eyes flickering. Flinging her napkin to the table, she rose, knocking over her chair. Her father and sister swung their heads in her direction. "Well, I think it's disgusting," she yelled. "All you care about is one thing. Your wife is barely gone and all you can think of is having a warm body next to you. It makes me sick. You're nothing but a pig . . . both of you!" She whirled around and ran from the room.

They stared after her for a moment, then looked at each other.

"*Both* of us?" Tom asked. "What warm body do you have next to you?"

Peggy felt herself flush. "I don't know what she means, Daddy."

"What's wrong with her? Why is she so . . . so angry all the time?"

"I don't know. She's just in a gazinga, I guess." Peggy actually had some ideas on the subject but she was much more interested now in her father's announcement. "Are you *really* going to get married?"

"Ah, Peg, eventually, I suppose. I didn't mean to imply I had someone in mind."

She was relieved. She wanted her father to be happy but not quite so soon; it would be an affront to her mother's memory. "Are you very lonely, Daddy?"

"Often. Are you?"

"Sometimes." But I have Jaret, she thought. Then she realized how selfish her thinking was. "Oh, Daddy, I think you *should* get married."

"Well, I suppose one of these days I'll start looking around. Not yet though. It just doesn't feel right yet. I guess I'll know when the time comes." He pulled at a slight fold in his neck. "Do you think I should make that clear to Claire?"

"I guess."

"I wish I understood her better. I used to, when she was little. Then something happened. I don't know what."

Peggy knew what. When Claire had arrived at dating age and become conscious of her looks it had made her angry, resentful and cold, and she had withdrawn from everyone. But Peggy didn't know how to explain it to her father without sounding patronizing. And what good would it do anyway? She decided to let it go. "She just has moods."

"Hmmm. She's such a self-sufficient girl."

"Woman," Peggy corrected him.

"What? Oh sure, woman. She just doesn't seem to need anyone. No friends, no boyfriends. Not like you. Who's the current one anyway?"

Again, Peggy felt a warmth creep up her neck. She stalled. "Current one?"

"Boyfriend." He grinned at her, winked.

"I'm not into boys right now. The boys around here are the pits."

"Well, it'll be different at college."

"Yeah. Should I get dessert?"

He nodded.

In the kitchen Peggy leaned her head against the refrigerator, her heart beating wildly. The thought of her father knowing about her and Jaret made her feel faint. She would have to be much nicer to Claire so there would be no danger of that. She couldn't imagine what he'd think if he knew and she sure as hell didn't want to find out.

It never occurred to her that if she'd been having a sexual relationship with a boy the thought of her father finding out would have made her feel just as faint.

13

July 14th

I was sixteen today. Happy Birthday to me. Big deal.
They gave me a cake and some clothes. Who needs it?
Oh, yeah, the Creep gave me a Swiss Army Knife.
Little does he know how handy it's gonna be. Ha!
She made such a big goddamn deal over the Creep
that you would have thought it was *his* birthday. Who
does she think he is anyway? Some kind of star? Well,
we'll just see who the star of this family is going to be!

And speaking of stars, the one that thinks she's the
biggest goddamn star of all is that frigging Jaret
Tyler. Talk about your big goddamn deals. Well, I

have news. The way she walks around you'd think she owned Gardener's Point or something. Eyes straight ahead, goddamn nose in the air, never giving you so much as a nod. Well, has that bitch got a surprise in store for her.

I've been watching her real close. I follow her whenever I can. It's real hard without wheels but I get around pretty good. Between my bike and Carter's car I do all right. Carter wanted to know why I was into following her and I told him I'd break his arm if he didn't stop being so goddamn nosy. He's so glad to have someone to hang around with he'd do whatever I say.

It's gonna be hard to get her alone. She's almost always with Peggy. I thought about getting them both but then I'd have to bring Carter in on it and that could be dangerous. He's too much of a jerk and would probably screw it all up. So I gotta settle on just Jaret. Anyway, I know that sooner or later I'll get her alone somewhere. One of these days she'll go into those woods alone. I hope. She's never done it yet . . . at least not since I've been watching, but I bet she does. When they go down there from her house they always walk since it's so close. When they go from Peggy's or someplace else they drive. I've seen them doing it a couple of times now. Christ! I'd like to tell the papers. What a riot. I can just imagine the reaction. I thought about sending anonymous letters to their parents but I'd screw everything up if I did. I'm gonna need that info later. Can't wait until I can tell *her* what I know. I can just picture her squirming away, begging me not to. I'll put that knife right up close to her throat and look right into those goddamn cold eyes of hers. She'll *have* to look at me then. I hate that frigging bitch. Soon.

14

They lay in their place in the woods. It was cool, the sun having dipped behind the trees an hour before. The remains of their picnic lunch were strewn around them, along with some books of poetry, notebooks and a radio. They'd spent the whole day in their private spot, earlier in bathing suits but now in shorts and shirts. And it had been lovely, relaxed, lazy. Yet something nagged at Jaret, an undefined tug slightly marring things. Peggy hadn't said or done anything unusual; but a part of her seemed distracted. Jaret had thought of asking if something was wrong but she hadn't wanted to ruin the day. But now, as it was ending, and Peggy seemed more distracted

97

more removed, Jaret decided to risk possible problems.

"Char," she said, touching Peggy's arm lightly, "something's bothering you, isn't it?"

Peggy smiled. "Oh, Jare, you know me so well."

Quoting, Jaret said, "Two souls with but a single thought, two hearts that beat as one."

"So true."

"Tell."

Now Peggy quoted: "It is not hard to find the truth. What is hard is not to run away from it once you have found it."

Jaret thought that over. "What truth?"

"The truth I'm trying to dodge. This is some humungus number, babe. I mean, I don't want to spoil things but I know I have to tell you sometime."

"Then tell me now, kid." She tried to sound casual like her mother always did. Inside she felt as though she were crumbling. What could it be? Didn't Peggy love her anymore? No, that couldn't be it. Not after today.

"Oh, Cree Cree, I don't know."

"You have to, Char. I mean, you know I won't let you alone until you do. I'll drive you up a wall, hassle you till you're bananas, make you gaga." Her voice rose, trying for fun, giving way to fear.

Peggy wasn't fooled. She took Jaret's hand. "I don't want to lay a heavy trip on you."

"C'mon. Remember this? 'If ever I said, in grief or pride,/I tired of honest things, I lied.' Edna St. Vincent Millay," said Jaret reverently.

"I remember. Okay. But, Jare, promise you won't get crazy and go into some kind of gazinga."

"No gazingas, I promise." She couldn't remember the last time she'd felt this apprehensive, fearful.

"Okay. Well, this is it . . . Mark McClinchie asked me out for Saturday night."

It *did* make Jaret feel crazy. Two years ago Peggy had dated Mark for a short time until he'd dropped her for Vilma Smith, a cheerleader. Peggy had told Jaret she'd been mad for him, brokenhearted when he'd split. If it had been anyone else but Mark it would have been different. Maybe.

"You hear me, Jaret?"

"Sure. What d'you expect me to say?"

"I dunno." Peggy shrugged. "Something."

"Something," she said sulkily.

"Oh, wow."

"Okay, I'm sorry. I guess I should expect people to ask you out. I guess it'll keep happening, huh?"

"I guess. You too."

"Yeah."

They were silent for a few moments, avoiding eye contact. Peggy fussed with the hem of her shorts, wondered for the thousandth time whether not shaving her legs was really doing anything for the Women's

Movement and thanked God she was blond. Finally, her mind whirled back to the problem at hand and she knew she had to go on. "Jare, I said yes."

"Huh?"

"To Mark. I said I'd go out with him." She bit the inside of her cheek. The last thing she wanted to do was hurt Jaret but she also wanted very much to go out with Mark McClinchie.

Jaret was stunned, speechless.

"Cree?" Peggy said softly.

Jaret had to get hold of herself. She didn't want to come off sounding like a jealous lover. Jealousy, she knew, was deadly; jealousy, however, is what she was feeling.

Peggy touched her arm. "Are you mad?"

"Sometimes you're not very swift, are you?"

"I wouldn't blame you if you were."

"Thanks a bunch." She could not keep the sneer out of her voice.

Peggy sat up, her back to Jaret. "Oh, wow."

Jaret sat up. "Well, what do you expect?" Now jealousy was replaced by anger.

"I dunno." It was going exactly as she'd expected. Terribly.

"I mean, it's not something to cheer about, you know. I love you. Why should I get off on you going out with someone else? That make sense?"

"It's just a date."

100

"No, it's *not* just a date, Peg. At least be honest about it."

"Uh-oh, watch out, folks. Lawyer at work!"

Jaret took Peggy by the shoulders and tugged her around so they faced each other. "Don't try and twist this. You were once hung up on Mark. Isn't that true?"

"I'm not now."

"Then why, may I ask, are you going out with him?"

"Let me ask *you* a question, Jaret."

Jaret wondered what Peggy was up to but signaled assent with a nod of her head.

"Do you love me *because* I'm a woman or in spite of it?"

"I don't get it," Jaret said, suspicious.

"I mean, do you wish I was a guy? Or you were a guy?"

"No. Why?" She was genuinely confused.

"Well, it would be easier, wouldn't it?"

"Easier?"

Peggy sighed. "Yes, easier. A lot easier than being . . . being . . ."

"A dyke?"

"Oh, don't. That's a disgusting word," Peggy said, making a face.

"Only the way *they* use it. It's like nigger. Black people say nigger about themselves to diminish the

101

power of the word."

"Spoken like a politician."

Jaret ignored the remark. "Anyway, to answer your question, I love you *because* you're a woman. How about you?"

"Oh, Jare. Sometimes it just brings me down. Sometimes I wish one of us was a guy."

Jaret was astonished. "Then we wouldn't be us. If you were a guy I wouldn't be interested."

"Oh, I know, that's the trouble. I don't know what I'm saying."

But, suspecting Peggy did know, Jaret chose to pursue the Mark issue instead. "What about this date with Mark?"

"What about it?"

Jaret pressed her lips together, both dimples appearing. "Look, if I *were* a guy and we were going together you wouldn't date someone else, would you?"

There was only one obvious answer to this question so Peggy tried ignoring it. "I'm curious. That's all."

"About him or the way you feel about him?"

"Both. Is that so hard to understand?"

"Yes. Somehow it is. I guess I thought you knew how you felt." Jaret hoped she wouldn't cry. "I mean, if you love me, Peg, then what is it you think you might feel for him?"

"I don't know, Jare. That's the whole point." Peggy sounded desperate. "Do you want me to break the date?"

Jaret knew the question was a terrible trap. If she said yes, which was what she wanted to say, Peggy would resent her for it. So she had to say no and be untrue to her feelings. She decided to explain the conflict to Peggy.

"Well, where does that leave me?" Peggy asked after hearing Jaret's dilemma.

"I don't know. We can't both be winners in this thing. It's the pits, isn't it?"

"*You're* making it the pits. I didn't think it would be such a humungus deal."

"Yes, you did," Jaret said.

"What's that supposed to mean?"

"C'mon, Peg . . . get honest."

Peggy jumped to her feet. "I *have* been honest, Jaret Tyler. I could have made up some story about Saturday night and you never would have known the difference. But no, I decided to tell you the truth and what do I get for it? A lot of hassling. Well, you can just go to hell." Quickly she turned and walked toward the path.

Jaret rose to her knees, started to call out, changed her mind. There was no point going on with it just then. They'd talk later. She sank back down on the blanket and looked around. The only thing she felt at the moment was annoyance at having to carry everything home alone. Maybe Peggy would come back. No, Jaret knew she would not. She was too angry. And, Jaret knew, too guilty. She hated that. It wasn't

103

right that Peggy should have to feel guilty about going out with Mark, if that's what she wanted. Was it? The thought made Jaret feel sick. Was it all going to end? As long as we're happy, she said in her mind. Damn Mark McClinchie.

Peggy put the car in gear and squealed out of Jaret's driveway. She couldn't remember when she'd been so mad. Certainly never at Jaret. Not like this. Sure, they'd had their disagreements, like any couple, but this was different.

She stopped at the light in the middle of town. A bunch of boys were hanging around the front of the Bee Hive, Chris Tyler among them. Feeling an inexplicable hatred for him, she turned away as he lifted his hand to wave. She didn't waste a second when the light changed. Three blocks later she began to shake her head, angry at herself for her ridiculous behavior. Really dumb, she thought. What did Chris have to do with anything anyway? Why take it out on him? It was Jaret she hated, not Chris. Hated? Oh, no. That was much too strong. It was Jaret she was mad at, annoyed with.

Turning into Barlow Terrace she realized she was headed toward Bianca's. She had to talk to someone and Bianca was the only possibility, the only one who knew and would understand.

As Peggy raised her hand to knock on the Chambers' door it opened. Bianca, outfitted in a long, purple-velvet gown with puffed sleeves and great expanses of skirt, and a rhinestone tiara which was almost lost in her hair, said in a booming voice: "'Small cheer and great welcome makes a merry feast.' Shakespeare. *Comedy of Errors.* Act three, scene one, line twenty-six." She bowed low.

"Aren't you hot?" Peggy asked.

Slowly, Bianca rose from her bow, one eyebrow arched. "You have no soul."

"None. Can I come in?"

"Of course, dear heart. You look a little peaky. What's wrong?" She took Peggy's arm, pressing too hard with her large hand, and guided her up the stairs to her room, closing the door after them. "Speak. What is it?"

Peggy dropped heavily into a beanbag chair, molding it to her shape.

"Jaret and I have had a humungus fight."

"Oh, dear. Do you want to tell me about it?" Bianca picked up a lacy fan from her desk and began to cool herself.

"Why don't you get out of those clothes?"

"Yes, I suppose I should." Grandly, she rose and walked to her closet, suddenly stopped, whirled around and stared at Peggy.

"What is it?"

105

"Oh, nothing." She walked back to her chair and sat down, picked up the fan.

"I thought you were going to change."

"I've changed my mind. Tell me about the fight, dear one."

"Oh, Bianca." Peggy began to cry, the tears running down her cheeks into the corners of her mouth.

Bianca was not one of the world's great comforters. Showing affection didn't come easily to her. She was awkward when hugging someone who was upset; her large hands pounded sympathy rather than patting it. It was as if she had no control over her strength, embarrassment rather than compassion leading the way. So she sat where she was, on the chair, on her hands, waiting for Peggy's crying to subside. "Maybe if you talk about it, Peg, it won't hurt as much," she said gently.

Peggy nodded. "Got a tissue?"

Grateful to be able to help somehow, Bianca leaped to her feet, purple train dragging behind her, ran from the room and was back in a moment with a box of tissues which she clumsily dropped in Peggy's lap. "Sorry," she said.

Peggy shook her head, not wanting Bianca to feel bad about her heavy-handed effort. "Thanks." She wiped her eyes, dabbed at her nose.

On the bed Bianca leaned against the colorful throw pillows. "Can you tell me about it now?"

"Yes, I think so."

"Take your time."

Slowly, Peggy filled her in on the events beginning with Mark McClinchie's phone call. When she finished she settled back and waited for some words of wisdom.

Bianca's fingertips tapped against each other in a praying position. "Well," she said, "I can understand how Jaret would feel. Like I would if Zach said he was having a date with someone else." She waved the fan quickly. A line of perspiration ran along her upper lip.

"I wish you'd get rid of those clothes, Bianca."

Bianca narrowed her blue eyes. "Just what do you mean by that?"

"By what?"

Bianca was dying of the heat. "All right, my friend, I'll trust you." She got up.

"Trust me?" Peggy was puzzled. "What are you talking about?"

"I am talking about changing my clothes which *you* so des-per-ate-ly want me to do."

"*I* desperately want you . . . Oh, no . . . oh, wow! I don't believe this." Peggy started to laugh.

"I see nothing funny in this matter." The fan went crazy.

Peggy controlled her laughter. "If it weren't so funny, so far out, I think I'd cry. You honestly think

107

I want to see you with your clothes off, don't you? Bianca, have you forgotten that I've known you six years and we've spent many nights together? I've seen you without your clothes a hundred times. Oh, wow! This is off the wall."

A reddish hue crept up Bianca's neck and flushed her cheeks.

"Besides," said Peggy, "do you think I'm interested in *all* females?"

"I thought . . . I don't know," she said, somewhat ashamed.

"No, I guess you don't. I thought you understood. I mean, are you interested in every *guy* you see?"

Bianca shook her head, some of her frizzy hair slapping her cheeks.

"Of course you aren't. I mean, where are you coming from anyway? I think I'd better go." Peggy started to get up and Bianca ran to her, pushing her back in the chair.

"Please, don't," she said, pleading. "I'm sorry . . . really. I didn't mean to hurt you, Peg. It's just all so confusing. First Jaret, now Mark. I'm all mixed up. And look, I'm going to change my clothes right now." She unbuttoned the tiny buttons which fronted the dress. "See. I'm taking off the dress."

Peggy smiled. Poor Bianca. She tried.

"Now," Bianca said, kicking the dress aside and going to her closet, "what are you going to do about Mark?"

"What do *you* think I should do?"

Bianca pulled on her jeans. "Maybe if you didn't have to wait until Saturday to go out with Mark you could find out how you feel, and then you and Jaret could, well, work things out."

"But I *do* have to wait until Saturday."

Slipping on a T-shirt that said SARAH BERNHARDT WAS A MONOPODE, she said, "Why?"

"What else can I do?" Peggy rolled the tissue into a ball.

"You can call him. Change the date. I thought you were liberated."

"I am but, I dunno, it's not like we're on such friendly terms."

"Friendly enough to go out," Bianca said, adjusting her tiara.

"Well, maybe. I'd better go." She made her way out of the beanbag chair.

"I loathe that thing," Bianca said, towering over her. "So undignified. But my mother bought it so what can a girl do?"

Peggy looked up at her. "Thanks for your help."

Bianca flushed again. "I'm sorry if I hurt you, Peg. I didn't mean to but it is hard to, you know, understand."

Peggy nodded and reached out. In turn, Bianca engulfed her and squeezed so hard Peggy thought she might faint. As she sensed the hammerlike hand coming toward her back, she wriggled out of Bianca's

109

grip. "Easy," she said.

"Oh, horrors! Did I squeeze too hard?" Bianca put the back of her hand to her forehead.

"It's okay. I'm just especially frail today."

"Thank heaven Zach is so big."

They both tried laughing but it didn't really work.

At home, in her room, Peggy stared at the telephone. She thought of calling Jaret but didn't know what she'd say. Nothing had changed.

Then she thought of calling Mark, as Bianca had suggested. Maybe things *would* be clearer if she could see him sooner. The thought of spending time with Jaret with the date hanging over them was not appealing. Of course, she could break the date completely. Maybe Jaret was right. How would Peggy feel if things were reversed? She tried to imagine Jaret going out with Pete Cross. She found she didn't like it much. There was no question in her mind that she would be jealous. So why was she doing this to Jaret? Just to satisfy some curiosity, heal some old wound, salve her ego? It was rotten. She picked up the phone and dialed. He answered.

"Mark," she said, "it's Peggy."

"Oh, hi."

"Listen, I'm calling about Saturday night."

"Yeah?" His voice was wary.

"I . . . I . . . well, could we make it tonight instead?" It was as though someone else had spoken. A ventriloquist.

"Tonight? Well, I dunno. What's wrong with Saturday? Can't you make it then?"

She took a chance. "No. My father made some humungus plans for me I didn't know about. Sorry." She wasn't being very nice, she knew. Short, abrupt. What would he answer? It was like rolling a pair of dice or turning a wheel of fortune.

"Oh. Tonight, huh?" There was a moment of silence, the static on the line sounding like fireworks to her. "Yeah, well, okay."

"Super."

"See you at seven."

"See you then." She hung up, not saying good-bye, not waiting for his. She had two hours to eat dinner and get ready. Although she hadn't planned it before dialing Mark's number, she felt certain that this was the best way, the only way. Now when she called Jaret in the morning Peggy would know what she felt, would be able to be clearer and more honest. She was confident she had done the right thing. One way or the other, by morning her relationship with Jaret would be changed; it would either be stronger or it would be over. As far as Peggy was concerned, those were the only two possibilities.

15

It was five o'clock when Jaret looked at her watch.
She'd been lying on the blanket for an hour and a
half since Peggy had left, thinking, perhaps uncon-
sciously waiting for her return. So when she heard a
twig snap behind her she didn't immediately turn,
convinced Peggy *had* come back. She listened to
some rustling sounds, then felt the presence of another human being and decided to turn. Alarmed,
she gave a small, sharp squeal.

"Oh," she said, "it's you. I thought it was . . ."

"Yeah, I know who you thought it was. Your girlfriend."

She didn't like the way he said *girlfriend*. There

was something snide about it. "What are you doing here?"

"You own this part of the woods or something?"

"It was a simple question. Chris with you?" She felt nervous and didn't know why. She tried to look past him, hoping he was not alone, again not understanding why. Just a feeling.

"Nobody's with me. We're alone."

Why did everything he said sound so menacing? She started to pick up things. "I was just leaving."

"I figured when I saw you sit up."

The implication was, obviously, that he'd been watching her. It gave her goose bumps. She tried for a casual tone. "Have you been around here long?"

"Long enough."

She continued to gather her things. Had he heard their fight? Seen them kiss, make love? The thoughts made her want to run, to get as far away from him as possible. The invasion of her privacy sickened her. But perhaps he'd only been there, behind a bush, a tree, for minutes, seconds even. What did *long enough* mean? "How long is long enough?" she asked cheerily, not looking at him.

He laughed strangely. "A few hours . . . more or less."

She was chilled. Sooner or later she would have to look at him; she couldn't go on picking up things and tossing them into the middle of the blanket forever.

113

Eventually, she would have to pass him. Forcing herself, she faced him. He seemed much taller, bigger than he had moments ago. There was an odd smile on his face, if one could really call it a smile. Don't be afraid, she told herself. Or at least don't let him see it. Take command. "Just what is it you want?"

"You really think you're hot shit, don't you?"

"If you must know," she said, now trying for humor, "I have actually never thought about myself that way." She smiled, staring straight at him. Something awful is going to happen, she thought.

"Yeah, well, I have. Thought about you that way."

"I see." But she did not. Not clearly. There was enough evidence for her to feel apprehensive; yet what was ahead was blurry. Bravado, she felt, was her only weapon. Turning away from him, she bent down and began pulling the corners of the blanket toward the center to make a satchel. After twisting the ends together, she rose, heaving the makeshift bag over her right shoulder. He was standing, waiting. "Well, so long," she said, taking a step in his direction.

He did not move, continued to smile, blue eyes piercing. "You're going nowhere."

Now apprehension gave way to fear and she could feel the thumping in her chest. Choices overwhelmed her. What would be the best move? Should she try to humor him, laugh it off, pretend it was all a joke?

114

Threaten him with police, parents? Or should she try and make a run for it? She knew that the first thing was to stall, delay, for time. "Oh, Richard," she said, "what's this all about?"

He made a sneering, hissing sound. "Richard? Why don't you call me Mid like anybody else?"

"I forgot. All right, Mid." Then quickly, buying minutes: "Why do they call you Mid? I always wondered that." Was it stupid to make him think she'd spent time thinking about him? Too late.

He narrowed his eyes, squinting at her. "Like in midsummer. You know, Mid Summers?"

"Oh, sure." She smiled. "I get it." The blanket over her shoulder was growing heavy. She wanted desperately to lower it but to do so, she knew, would be an indication that she was staying. He was very close but there was still room for her to take a few steps in the direction of leaving. She would have to try.

"I said you're not going."

Quickly, "And I asked you what this is all about?"

"That's for me to know and you to find out." His eyes were boring into hers.

She could feel beads of sweat forming above her lip. They itched. Her arm ached. "I have to go home," she said softly, plaintively.

"Tough." He reached into his pocket and pulled out his knife, opened it to the largest blade.

115

Was he going to kill her? She felt like giggling.

"Drop the blanket," he commanded.

Jaret thought to do that would seal her fate. "Why, Mid? What do you want?"

He took a step closer and pressed the knife to her throat. Through his teeth he repeated his order.

She thought she might gag, swallowed noisily, allowed the bundle to slip from her grasp.

"Now open up the blanket and move all the shit out of it."

"Why?"

With his knifeless hand he smashed her across the face, sending her tumbling backward, falling. "Don't ask why about everything," he screamed. "Do what I tell you."

She lay on the ground, face stinging, back aching. There was no question in her mind now; her life was on the line. Mid Summers was crazy. Her options all seemed to meld together, leaving her with nothing. She wanted her mother. Tears made her vision go out of focus. She blinked them away and saw that Mid was opening the blanket, kicking books, radio, notebook out of the center.

"Get over here on this blanket. Move."

She moved, crawled on all fours, the few feet to the blanket where she sat curled into herself, every part of her shaking.

"Lie down."

116

Oh, my God, she thought, astonished that she hadn't thought of it before. It was so clear. Mid Summers was going to rape her. It was as though her heart actually stopped beating for a moment. A sharp pain ripped through her side. He'd kicked her.

"I said lie down, bitch."

She rolled over, clutching at a bottom rib. Was it broken, cracked? Oh, God. The pain was horrendous.

His voice split the air around them. "On your back."

She obeyed, painfully.

"Now take off your shorts." He fell to his knees next to her, the knife pointed toward her throat.

Last year in school there'd been a lecture on what to do in case of rape. She hadn't really listened; it couldn't happen to her. Should she try to talk him out of it? Submit peacefully? But she knew him, could identify him. Wouldn't he kill her afterward? Would talking make it worse? She had to give it a try. "Mid, please don't do this. You'll get in a lot of trouble."

He laughed. "No, I won't. Ace in the hole." He laughed again. "Take off the shorts."

Ace in the hole? What did he mean? She asked.

"Later. Take off the shorts and quit the rapping."

She felt the knife point dig into her neck. As she began slowly to unbutton her shorts she thought of another tack. Flattery. "You're a good-looking guy,

117

Mid. You don't have to do this. Lots of girls would be glad to do it with you."

"I said to shut up." This time he hit her with a closed fist.

The sound of flesh and bone connecting with flesh and bone magnified inside her head to a deafening pitch. The intensity of noise almost obliterated pain. Not quite. She had never felt anything like it. In a moment she tasted blood. Salty. Thought, as she knew it, was gone. Something was happening to her shorts but she couldn't explain it to herself. It was like waking in a strange place and, for a moment, not knowing where you are. She was being pushed, pulled, scrambled. There was a loud sound far away. It was familiar but she couldn't place it. When she felt something on her upper thigh she identified the sound. Ripping. Her shorts. And what she felt on her thigh was flesh. His hand.

"Open your legs." His voice was tight, caught in his throat.

Her brain told her to obey but she didn't seem to know how. She saw the fist come toward her. She moved too slowly and it caught her squarely on the bridge of her nose. There was a crunch, then warm, gushing liquid flowed over her lips, chin. Blood. Pain.

"You don't learn, do you?"

His voice sounded as though it were coming from a

great distance or through the small end of a megaphone. She'd heard something like this before, when she'd had a fever. Mama. Her legs were being spread apart, wrenched. Broken? Then he was on top of her. His weight was crushing, his breath warm and sour in her face. Nausea fought pain for control.

Time passed. Years, she thought. Was she an old woman now? Abruptly, painfully, he entered her. She could not help crying out. The knife slid down the side of her neck, cold, pointed. Was she cut? He began to move. I cannot believe this is happening, she thought. There's nothing I can do. That was the worst, the hardest thing to understand, accept. There was nothing she could do.

"I hate your guts," he whispered.

Why then? she wondered apathetically. His movement continued. Her head was turned to the side. Breathing became difficult. Month after month passed. Staring at the landscape, she wondered why the seasons didn't change. Where was the snow? She longed for snow, cool, white. Snow would stop the burning inside. She felt her body rock as Mid's movements quickened. Would she break apart? Explode into pieces of flesh, bone, blood, flying through the air, sticking to the trees, bushes?

Days went by before she recognized the stillness. Nothing was moving. Then a wayward leaf skipped by on a small breeze. She blinked her eyes. Mid was

119

lying across her, his head down next to her neck. He was motionless, his breathing echoing in her ear like the roar of a lion. What now, she wondered. Will he kill me? The thought was simple, dispassionate. Deep emotions were impossible; numbness was the prevalent feeling.

Slowly, Mid raised himself, rolled off to the side. Jaret heard him rustling with his clothes, the sound of a zipper. He cleared his throat, spit into the grass. "I want you to listen," he said. "You hear?"

When she did not respond quickly, he punched her in the stomach. She vomited onto the blanket, choking.

"Shit," he said. "That stinks." He pulled her off the blanket, onto the grass. There were strings of vomit on her cheek, mixing with the blood.

"You're not such hot shit now," he said. "I wish I had a mirror. Look at me when I talk, you bitch."

She opened her eyes. He knelt next to her, the knife gripped in his hand, pointed in her direction. She felt nothing.

"Now listen. If you tell anybody I'm gonna tell about you and Peggy Danziger, understand? I'm gonna tell your mother and father and everybody. Get it?"

She got it and it made her smile, though to do so was terribly painful. Still, she couldn't help it.

"What's so goddamn funny?" His mouth pulled

120

sideways into a grimace.

Even in her bleary state she understood enough not to tell him that her mother already knew. This was his "ace in the hole." And this would keep her alive. She stopped smiling and whispered, "Nothing . . . funny."

"Good. So remember: You talk and I talk." Then he giggled maniacally. "I guess you gotta tell them something, don't you?" A chortle. "Okay, you tell them an old guy about forty did it. Yeah. Tall, real fat and ugly." He warmed to his description. "Red hair and . . . red beard. A scar here." He pointed to his right eye, drew his finger down his cheek. "Say he was wearing jeans and a green sweat shirt, sleeves cut off. A broken nose. Yeah. Tell them that. If you don't, I'll tell everything. I've been watching you two for a long time now. I know everything you do. Got it?"

Aching, she nodded.

"Just to make sure you do," he said.

The punch got her right on the point of her chin. She went out.

16

Kay poured herself and Bert another drink. She
didn't really want it but it passed the time. If Jaret
wasn't back when they finished, they'd eat dinner
without her. Kay looked at her watch for the hun-
dredth time. Seven thirty-five.

"Why don't you call Peggy?" Bert asked.

"Chris said he saw Peggy alone around three
thirty." She ran her small hand through the curls.

"I know, but maybe she knows where Jaret went."

What confused them both was Jaret's car in the
driveway. And, of course, she had never been this
late without calling. Kay wondered why she was de-
laying the call to Peggy. Was it because she didn't

want to be your typical worrywart mother? Well, hell, she thought, I *am* your typical worrywart mother. She put down her drink and walked to the phone and dialed.

Claire answered.

Kay asked for Peggy and was told she was on a date. A date? Why would Peggy be on a date? When Kay hung up she was more concerned than ever but she couldn't explain that to Bert. She damned herself for not having already told him about Jaret and Peggy. Now was not the time. Something was very wrong. She knew it intuitively. "I think we should call the police, Bert."

"At quarter of eight? I think we should eat dinner." He wanted to sound casual, unconcerned. For Kay. In truth, he was terribly worried. It wasn't like Jaret to do something like this.

"I can't," she said.

Chris came into the room. "Mom? What's happening?" He was sure too that something wasn't right. He hadn't mentioned that Peggy had ignored him that afternoon, but to him it was a sure sign that something was goofy. How could he explain that to his parents?

"No news," Kay said.

"You call Bianca?" Chris asked.

She nodded. "Peggy dropped by but not Jaret."

"Maybe . . . maybe you should call the police."

123

"Not yet," Bert said. "After all, it's not as though it's midnight or something." He sounded more confident than he felt.

"Where would *you* look, Chris?"

Chris felt uneasy. Should he tell them he'd seen Jaret and Peggy together in the woods?

The ringing of the phone made them all jump. Kay answered. It was Bianca.

"Can anyone hear me?" Bianca asked, whispering.

"Just me." Kay's hand was sweaty on the phone.

"I know you know about them—Peggy and Jaret— and I've been thinking, well, God they're going to kill me, but I know you're worried, Mrs. Tyler."

"Yes, we are." She wanted to shake the phone, shake Bianca. What was it she knew?

"Well, they had a fight. Peggy told Jaret that she was going out with Mark McClinchie and they fought. Peggy left Jaret there."

"Where?" Kay shouted.

"In the woods. They have this special place they go in the woods near your house."

"Where is it? This place?"

"Gee, I don't know. I've never been there. But Peggy would know. Only she's not home. She went out with Mark tonight instead of Saturday night. I guess it's my fault."

Kay didn't bother to ask *what* was her fault. "Do you know where Peggy and Mark might be?"

"They could be anywhere. I really don't think there's anything wrong. I mean, Jaret wouldn't do anything dumb, you know. She's probably just thinking, getting her head together."

"Yes, probably." Kay thanked Bianca for calling and turned toward her husband and son. Instinctively, she knew her daughter wasn't just thinking. Instinctively, she knew action was needed. "I think she's in the woods," Kay said calmly. "And I think we'd better look for her."

The tone of his wife's voice brought Bert to his feet. "What is it, Kay?"

"I'm not sure but I think we'd better hurry."

"I think that's where she is too," Chris said.

Kay looked at him for a moment, wondered what he knew, decided to deal with that later. "Flashlights. It'll be dark soon. Quick."

It was black now. When Jaret had awakened there was still a faint light streaking through the trees. She had no idea what time it was or how long she'd been awake. She had wrapped herself in the unsoiled part of the blanket, her head turned away from the drying vomit. Once she had tried sitting, but the pain was too great. It was getting colder and colder and her teeth began to chatter. She thought of her mother, Peggy, a movie, a book. Anything but the event

125

which had gotten her to this point. She was trying to remember the lines of a Millay poem and was stuck on the fourth one when she heard it. Someone calling. A woman's voice. And a man's. A name. *Her* name. She opened her mouth to answer; nothing came out but a tired saliva bubble. Her voice was imprisoned in her throat as if she were in a dream.

In the distance something was flickering. Even with her eyes swollen almost shut she could make out that it was a light of some sort. She tried to call out again as her name was repeated. Her mouth formed a word. *Mama.* It was a whisper.

"Jaret?" Kay called.

"Jaret?" It was Bert.

"Jaret?" Chris bellowed.

They were coming closer. Then there was nothing. No sound, no name, no light.

Jaret panicked and pushed herself up on an elbow. Pain shot through her. "Mama," she said softly. "Mama." A little louder. She had enough strength for one more. "Mama!" It came out howling as she fell back down on the ground.

"Oh, my God." She heard Kay's voice.

Then there was running, snapping twigs, perhaps falling. And suddenly her eyes burned as a light shone on them.

"Oh, Jesus!" It was her father. "Oh, Jesus God."

"Jaret. Jaret, baby," Kay said.

126

"Oh, Jare," Chris whispered.

They were all around her. She couldn't see them clearly but she could feel them, sense them, and now she knew she was safe. She let go then, slipping once again into oblivion, a place of safety.

Bert gagged from the smell of vomit as he carefully lifted his daughter in his arms.

"Shall I help, Dad?"

"Not yet." Bert struggled to his feet, Jaret's weight almost buckling him. He steadied himself, held her across his arms, as he looked into her battered, bruised face, dried blood everywhere. "Oh, my God, my baby," he said, "my poor baby." Tears streaked his cheeks. "Guide me with the flashlight."

They stumbled and tripped back through the woods, Kay leading, holding the flash in front of Bert; Chris brought up the rear, ready to help his father at any moment. Except for their crunching steps, the slapping and scraping of bushes as they passed, the only noise coming from the grim procession was the sound of weeping. Jaret alone was silent.

17

"Hiya, toots."

Jaret heard her mother's voice but with her eyes puffed nearly closed it was hard to see her. She felt a hand holding hers and tried to press it, but nothing happened.

"How do you feel, Jaret?" Her father's voice.

Why were they standing around her bed? Why couldn't she see them? There was a sudden, shocking flood of memory: Mid, the beating, the rape, her rescue. Logic told her she was in a hospital. She remembered her father had asked her a question. What was it?

"You're going to be all right, kid," Kay said.

She wanted to answer but she'd forgotten how. It was easier to sleep.

When Kay and Bert returned to the waiting room Peggy, whom Kay had summoned, was sitting with Chris. She jumped to her feet as they entered.

"How is she? Can I see her?"

Kay put a hand on Peggy's shoulder. "She's sleeping, Peg. But she did open her eyes for a bit, much as she could, poor kid." She lost control, began to cry.

Bert put his arm around her and Chris shoved his hands in his pockets and began to pace.

"My father's here," Peggy said. "He's talking to Dr. Rosner. What happened? Do you know? Is she hurt badly? Is anything broken?"

The barrage of questions brought Kay out of herself. Poor Peggy. She too needed comforting, reassuring. "We're not completely sure, Peg. It's obvious that she suffered a terrible beating and maybe . . ." Kay couldn't finish the sentence. The fact that Jaret's shorts had been torn away indicated she might have been raped. Tests were being done.

"And maybe what?" Peggy asked.

No one answered. Bert lit a cigarette. Chris stood staring out the window. Kay plucked the cigarette from Bert's fingers and he lit another.

If only, Peggy kept saying to herself. If only.

129

As Dr. Danziger and Elliot Rosner entered, the group moved toward them expectantly. Tom shook hands with Bert and gently touched Kay's shoulder.

"Have you seen her?" Dr. Rosner asked.

Kay nodded.

"It looks a lot worse than it is. What I mean is, it's not critical. No internal bleeding. Only her nose and one rib are broken. She'll be all right. Physically."

Kay's eyes widened.

"I'm sorry. Don't be alarmed," Dr. Rosner went on. "I'm saying this all wrong. It's just that this so rarely happens around here. I was thinking of her psyche. Our suspicions have been confirmed. She's been raped."

"Oh, my God." Kay sucked in her breath.

Bert took a step backward, as though he'd been punched.

Turning his back on them all, Chris tightly wrapped his arms around himself as if to keep from fracturing. Tom Danziger put an arm around his daughter and held her close, grateful it had not been Peggy, guilty at such a thought but knowing it was a normal reaction.

Dr. Rosner continued. "The police should be here any minute. Of course, I had to report it. I tried to stall them, tell them you'd talk in the morning, but you know how it is."

"They're not going to try to talk to Jaret tonight,

are they?" Kay asked.

"No. I won't let them. Do you suppose she knows who it was?"

"I have no idea," said Kay.

He was about to ask Peggy when Chief Edward Foster and Sergeant Jack Leden entered. There were introductions, expressions of sympathy.

"Now then," said Chief Foster, when the amenities were over, "I think the girl here should be excused before we begin."

Kay felt herself bristle. "And what about the boy?" She indicated Chris.

"No, he can stay." The chief ran a fleshy hand over his balding head.

"He's three years younger than she."

"Huh?" Foster was confused.

Bert squeezed Kay's arm. "Not now," he said softly.

She nodded. Now was not the time to react to sexism. "Well, Peg is eighteen. I think it's up to her."

"It might get rough, so to speak," Foster said.

"I'm staying," Peggy said.

"Well, come to think of it, you're her good friend. You might be helpful, after all." He adjusted the glasses on his long nose. "Now, in your own words, please tell me what happened."

Kay and Bert told what they knew, alternating, each helping the other when emotions threatened to

131

take over. When they were finished, Foster turned to Peggy.

"So then, you were the last one to see her before she was assaulted, right?"

"Yes, I suppose so." Guilt invaded her.

"What's the name of her boyfriend?"

"What does that have to do with anything?" Kay asked.

"Pardon?" said Foster.

"Why do you want to know about a boyfriend? She was horribly beaten. It has nothing to do with a boyfriend."

"Pardon, Mrs.," Foster said, "but you're out of your element here, so to speak. The girl was raped and we have to find the perpetrator. Now, please, let me do my job."

"This is a crime of violence," Kay went on, "not a sexual one."

Foster cackled, took a swipe at his nose with thumb and forefinger. "Well, if rape ain't sexual then I don't know what is."

"Well, I have news for you," Kay persisted, her voice rising. "It ain't sexual. It's aggressive and it's violent and it's based on hatred of women, not desire for them."

Bert stepped forward. "Please, Kay. Let Chief Foster do what he has to."

"Thank you, sir." The chief nodded toward Bert.

132

"But it's absurd to think some boy did this out of lust."

"Howsoever, I still want the name of her boyfriend."

"She doesn't have one," said Peggy. She wanted desperately to shout that she was Jaret's lover; yet she hoped also that no one else would find out, especially her father.

"No steady, huh?" said Foster. "Well, who'd she date?"

"She used to go out with Peter Cross," Bert said.

"Peter wouldn't do something like that," Peggy said. But who would?

"Of course not," Kay said.

"You'd be surprised who'd do what." Foster's cheek was twitching. "We'll check out the Cross boy." He turned to Dr. Rosner. "When can we see the girl?"

"You'll be able to see her in the morning."

"You know," the chief turned back to Kay and Bert, "we've never had one of these before. Course everybody's getting wilder these days, so to speak."

Kay wondered if she was hearing things. Was he implying *they* were somehow at fault? Or that Jaret was?

"They don't have the morals they used to," Foster said.

"Who doesn't?" Bert asked through clenched teeth.

Kay knew she hadn't been hearing things.

133

"Oh, kids, parents, everyone," he said.

"Which kids?" Bert's hands balled into fists at his sides.

Foster grinned toothily. "All kids, Mr. Tyler. All of 'em."

Kay couldn't contain herself. "Are you trying to make this Jaret's fault, Chief?"

"Fault? I never said nothing about fault. 'Specially hers."

And, of course, he hadn't, directly. There was nothing more to be said.

Foster shook his head. What fools a man met in his line of work. He motioned to Leden to follow him as he lumbered out of the room.

When they were gone Dr. Rosner urged the Tylers and Peggy to go home. It was after one o'clock in the morning.

"But what if she wakes up?" Peggy wished she would. She needed to see her, be with her, hold her.

"She's sedated," Rosner said. "She'll sleep through the night. Come back tomorrow."

Driving home with her father, Peggy wondered how he'd react when the truth came out. And she wondered how *she* would react when he disowned her. What would her mother have said, done?

Claire was waiting up and fussed over them both

134

in her mother-hen fashion, trying to get them to eat and drink something, asking endless questions. Neither wanted anything but to go to bed.

Alone, in her room, Peggy could not stop blaming herself. If only the whole Mark McClinchie thing hadn't come up she and Jaret would never have fought and Jaret would never have been in the woods alone. The worst thing about it was that it had happened because of Mark McClinchie. He was the pits!

How could she ever have been hung up on him? Never had she seen anyone so in love with himself. In the living room, before they left, he wouldn't keep his eyes from the mirror. And all during the evening, every chance he got, he glanced in every possible reflecting surface. But the most humungus part was that he never stopped talking about himself. By the time she feigned sick, at about ten thirty, he had not asked her one question about herself. She let him kiss her at the door, not completely sure why. Perhaps as a test, although she didn't need one. Nevertheless, it couldn't hurt to be absolutely sure. It wasn't a terrible kiss; it just wasn't anything. She'd felt nothing except, perhaps, amusement. It was obvious from his performance—the way he took her in his arms, bent her backward slightly—that Mark thought he was a great lover. She had hoped Jaret would be able to see the humor in it all. But the joke had quickly faded when she entered her house and saw the faces of her father and Claire, who were waiting for her.

She kept going over the hours from the moment she'd left Jaret to the moment Kay told Peggy they'd found her. She couldn't stop wondering what she'd been doing when it happened. If only she'd called Jaret instead of Mark. If Kay had told her Jaret wasn't back yet . . . Oh, what was the use of this? It had happened.

The words startled her. She hadn't allowed herself to think about the terrible thing Jaret had experienced. Preoccupied with her own part in it, she hadn't thought about the horror Jaret must have felt. My God! Peggy felt so selfish and self-involved. Was she any better than Mark?

But even now she couldn't let her mind focus on what must have taken place. It was a shock to learn she was such a coward. She promised herself she wouldn't let Jaret see that side of her. No matter what, she would be brave for Jaret, help her get through this thing.

There was a soft knock at the door.

"Come in," Peggy said.

"I saw your light," said Claire.

"I can't sleep."

"I know. Neither can I. It's terrible, isn't it?"

Peggy nodded.

"I keep thinking it could have been you." Claire pushed her glasses back up on the bridge of her nose.

136

"I didn't think of that." Perhaps she wasn't as selfish as she thought.

"Really? It was the first thing that came to my mind. The second was that it's all going to come out."

"What is?"

"Your deviant relationship." Claire leaned against the woodwork around the door, feet crossed at the ankles.

"Why should it?"

"Oh, it just will. You'll see. Especially if they catch him. Things have a way of leaking. Dirty laundry and all that." Her fingers fluttered around the bottom edge of her hair, trying to shape it.

"I don't see that what happened to Jaret has anything to do with us."

"Well, you don't see anything, do you?"

"What's that supposed to mean?" Peggy threw back the covers and drew up her knees.

"Lift the scales from your eyes, why don't you? I thought you were supposed to be so damn bright."

"Get to the point, if you have one," Peggy said impatiently.

"It's clear to me that what you've done is to make Jaret a surrogate mother. It's a dependency problem at the root. Still, it's revolting." Claire chewed on her lip.

"You can't stand it that two people might just love each other, can you?"

Claire flinched. "Lesbianism is immature, Peggy."

"Oh, stick it in your gazinga."

Ignoring this, Claire went on. "At any rate, when it comes out, I hope you'll deny it."

Peggy looked at her sister quizzically.

"Nobody can prove it, you know, and it would kill Daddy." Seeing Peggy's surprise, Claire said, "I never would have told him."

"You're revolting."

"I'm revolting. Ha! Some nerve. Well, anyway, if I were you I'd stay out of it. Away from Jaret." She took a bite of her thumbnail.

"Well, you're *not* me." She wished Claire would go.

"I suppose it was some boy Jaret led on," Claire said.

Peggy was shocked. "How can you say that?"

"It's usually the girl's fault, you know. Freud says—"

"Maybe if you read less Freud and more Brownmiller you'd know better."

Claire dismissed this with her nail-bitten hand. "Oh, don't tell me about that paranoiac, Susan Brownmiller."

"She not a paranoiac. *You* are."

Claire stiffened. "Why do I waste my time with you? What do you know about abnormal psychology?"

"Everything, because I *am* abnormal . . . remember?" she said angrily. "And I'm psycho too. See!" She pushed herself to a standing position and began jumping around the bed, her eyes crossed, mouth twisted, strange guttural noises coming from deep within her.

"Oh, stop it." Claire chewed on a cuticle.

Breathless, Peggy let herself fall onto the mattress. She lay quite still, listening to her heartbeat.

"Sometimes I think you're a schizophrenic," Claire said.

Sometimes I think you're an ass, Peggy wanted to say, but decided there was no point. Instead she said, "Claire, do you blame my relationship with Jaret on *her?*"

"Yes."

"Don't. I think you should know that I declared myself first. If I hadn't, nothing ever would have happened between us." She did not say that Claire had given her the idea.

"You'll live to regret it," Claire said, and left the room.

"Thanks a lot," Peggy said to the closed door. "You're a real sister."

Chris switched on his black lights, lit some incense, put on his stereo earphones and stretched out on the

139

bed. The Rolling Stones would help him think.

He was sure if that turkey, Chief Foster, couldn't find who'd beaten and raped Jaret, that he and his friends could. In the morning he'd get Roger and Mid and Steve and Tony and they'd make a plan. It wouldn't be hard. All that was needed was a little patience, some legwork and some of the guy's own medicine. He could see himself beating the hell out of the guy. And, boy, would Mid ever give it to him! They could probably find the freak by afternoon. The thing was, he wanted to get to him before Foster did.

Then it occurred to Chris for the first time. Jaret would *tell* who it was. Of course! As soon as she woke up, could talk, she'd tell. Why hadn't he realized that before? But maybe she didn't know; maybe it was a stranger. Still, she could give a description. Suddenly he sat up. The clock said two thirty. He had to stay awake because the alarm was broken. As soon as it was light he'd go to the hospital, sneak in and get to Jaret's room. He had to be the first one to talk to her.

If his suspicions about Jaret and Peggy were true, then the freak who did this thing to Jaret probably made it a forever. Now she would *never* want to be with a man. She'd really hate them. He stood up, took off the phones and started walking around his room. Anger kept him moving. When he found the guy, and he was confident he would, he was going to

140

make mincemeat out of him. With a little help from his friends.

Kay stared into the black of the room, listening to Bert toss from side to side. She desperately wanted a cigarette. Sitting up, she dropped her feet over the side of the bed and felt around in the darkness for her slippers.

"What are you doing?" Bert asked.

"Looking for my slippers."

"Turn on the light."

"You've got to get some sleep."

"Why?"

Good question. She turned on the light.

"I just can't believe it," Bert said. "It's something you read about but you never think it's going to happen to someone you know, your own kid."

"I know." She patted his hand. "I want to get a cig, Bert." She went to the closet.

"You smoke too much," he said automatically.

She ignored it.

"Do you think she'll be all right?" he asked. "I mean, you know, psychologically?"

"Shanmuysnelpahulb," Kay said from inside the closet.

"What? I can't hear you."

She poked her head around the door. "I said, she

may need help."

"Oh. What are you doing in there?"

"Looking for my cigarettes. I know I put them in my jacket. I know it. You know what that means, don't you?"

Bert sighed. "Yes, Kay, I do."

"They're doing it again. It's a plot. They're trying to drive us crazy. I think the cigarettes and matches are the leaders—they do it more than the others."

"You don't need a cigarette," he said impatiently.

"Oh, but I do, kid. I do." She disappeared again.

With his finger Bert traced the pattern of a rose on the sheet, listening to the banging and slamming coming from the closet. Then he turned toward Kay's side of the bed. There, on her night table, behind a copy of *Free and Female*, were her cigarettes and matches.

"Kay," Bert yelled. "Kay!"

"Huh?" Her curly head emerged from the closet.

Bert held up the cigarettes.

Sheepishly, she returned to the bed and took them from him. "I know I put them in my gray jacket pocket."

"Sure you did."

"Someday all the inanimate objects in this house will rise up and kill me." She got back in bed, pulled up the sheet, lit her cigarette and inhaled deeply.

"What will kill you are those cigarettes."

142

"I know, I know." And she did. She'd stop soon.

They were silent for a few moments. Then Bert said, "I keep wondering if this thing is going to turn her against men."

Kay felt a stab of guilt. She knew she should tell him about Peggy but somehow she just couldn't. The rape was enough for him to handle. But was he really so fragile, so weak, that he couldn't take it? Take what? Or was it something else?

"What do you think, Kay?"

She looked into her husband's clear, open eyes. Innocent, she thought. Why do I want to protect him? And from what? "I don't know, kid. I just don't know." A small white lie.

"And there's another thing." He pulled at the beard around his mouth. "I keep wondering . . . Oh, hell." He waved away his thoughts.

"Tell me," she urged.

"Do you suppose it was . . . the first time for her?"

Kay remembered her conversation with Jaret the first night they'd discussed lesbianism. She'd asked Jaret about her relationship with Peter and Jaret had implied they'd had intercourse. Kay remembered too how she'd gone to her room afterward and cried, realizing her daughter was no longer a child.

"Kay, did you hear me?" Bert interrupted her thoughts.

143

"Yes, I heard." Should she tell him about that conversation?

"Well, what do you think?"

"She's eighteen," Kay said noncommittally. "Who knows?" She was a coward, after all.

"Well, I hope to hell she wasn't a virgin. I never thought I'd say something like that but if this is her first experience it might warp her forever. Make her frigid . . . or worse."

Kay wondered what *worse* was to him but was afraid to ask, to hear the answer. She squeezed his shoulder. "Look, Bert, it's bound to have an effect on her but Jaret's a pretty together kid. I mean, with our help and professional help, if she needs it, I don't think it'll shape her life. Whatever she is now will probably prevail." Nice double-talk, she thought. But it was true, in a way.

"I could kill the bastard," Bert said suddenly. "I really could kill him. I swear, Kay, if he walked in here now I don't think I'd be responsible for my actions. I keep seeing her lying there, her eyes swollen and black and the blood, the mess. Oh, God. What kind of a man could do that?"

"A sick one," she said.

"A monster. They'd better get him . . . they'd just better get him. Do you suppose she knew him?"

A chill ran through Kay. "I think not. If she had, he probably would have killed her."

144

"I hadn't thought of that. I hope she can give a good description."

"Listen, kid, I don't want to sound like something out of a B movie but we do have a big day tomorrow and we should try to sleep."

"You're right."

She snapped off the light. Without a word they turned toward each other, intertwining. It had been a long time since they'd gone to sleep that way. It felt good.

18

July 23rd

Well, I did it. I got that bitch. I guess she knows what's
what now. I really let her have it. There was blood
all over the place. I got some on my shirt so I ripped
it up and threw it away. The Old Lady asked me what
happened to it and I told her to shove it. She asked if
I was in a fight and I said yeah, I was. Some fight!
Some fun! I was real tired so I stayed home and
watched a cruddy TV program. That bitch better not
talk. She won't. She knows that if she does I'll tell
everything I know about her and that other bitch.
Always have an ace in the hole. That's my philosophy.
Well, I'm going to bed now. I'm tired but I feel good.
Got a lot accomplished. Hot shit!

19

Chris tried not to breathe. Inside the closet, he listened to hear if the hall was clear. He'd jumped into the closet when he'd heard voices, footsteps, coming from another corridor. The people he'd heard had passed the door moments ago; now he had to be sure that there was no one else. It was very quiet. Slowly, he opened the door, stepped past some mops and peered out. Nothing. He closed the door behind him and on sneakered feet ran quickly down to the end. Jaret was in Room 271. The last door was marked 252. He'd gone the wrong way! Breathing came hard, his pulse quickened, heartbeat accelerated. Flattening himself against the wall, he waited, listened. It was quiet except for the sound of labored breathing from 252.

Sidling along the wall he made his way back down the corridor, passing his old hiding place without incident. Then he heard voices. They were coming toward him. Frantically, he looked around. There was a women's bathroom and two regular rooms. He chose the bathroom, thinking at six thirty in the morning it would be empty. He was wrong. Taking a quick look under the stalls he saw that two were occupied. He ran into a third, locked it, sat on the seat and put his feet up against the door. Sweat ran down his face and he wiped at it with his sleeve. How would he ever explain it if he was caught? Someone might think *he* was a rapist. A toilet flushed. Then a second one. To him his breathing sounded like a great whooshing noise and he tried to quiet it, listening as the two women greeted each other, washed their hands, chatted. Then he heard them leave and slowly let his feet slide down the door to the floor.

Now he had a real problem. Once leaving the confines of the stall he would be, for at least three seconds, vulnerable to anyone coming in. And even if he made it to the door safely, what then? There could be someone in the hall. He had to chance it. There was no other way.

Heart drumming in his chest, he opened the stall and made a sprint for the outside door. He put his ear against the wood, heard nothing and opened it. The hall was empty. As quickly as possible, he ran the rest of the distance. At the end of the corridor he saw the room. 271. Again, he listened at the door. The room sounded quiet. He took the moment.

Standing breathless, his back against her door, he could not see Jaret's face but he could hear her breathing. It was not unlike the breathing he'd heard outside 252. On tiptoe he made his way across the room and looked down at her. He sucked in his breath, unprepared for what he saw. It was much worse than he'd remembered. Perhaps it was the daylight streaking through the windows, making everything look especially harsh. She looked awful, broken. It made Chris more determined than ever.

He touched her shoulder. She stirred but didn't waken. Carefully, he tapped her again and watched as her eyes flickered open a crack, trying to see past the swollen, blackened flesh.

"Jaret," he whispered, "it's me, Chris."

She made a small sound.

"Jare, can you hear me? It's me, Chris."

"Chr," she said, barely audible.

"Yeah, Chris. How are you, kid?"

Her tongue poked out slowly between her parched, cracked lips; she swallowed, tried to nod, to tell him she was okay, but couldn't.

"Listen, Jare, I don't have much time and I'm not supposed to be here but you got to tell me. I'll explain it all later, okay? Jaret, who did it?"

149

"Chr," she said again.

"Yeah, it's Chris," he said patiently. "Do you understand what I'm asking you, Jare? The nurses and doctors and everybody are gonna be in here soon and I'm gonna have to split so if you could just answer me. . . . I need to know before that turkey Foster gets here. Who did it, Jare?"

She opened her mouth again, licked at her lip, made a sound.

"Water? Do you want water?"

"Mmmm," she said.

Feverishly, he looked around the room. On the table, on the other side of her bed, was a pitcher and glass. He ran to it, bumping the end of the bed. Jaret gave a small cry.

"Oh, wow, I'm sorry," he said. He poured the water, spilling some on the sheet, floor, table. Then he brought the glass to her lips but she was lying too flat to drink it. He whimpered with frustration and shifted from foot to foot. It was as if he'd suddenly become stupid. What to do? He realized he would have to lift her head. Slipping one hand under her neck, he slowly raised her. She made a noise and, frightened that he was hurting her, he lowered her back to the pillow.

"Chr," she said, "wahder."

There was no way he could stop the tears that filled his eyes. He wanted to scream, to throw the glass across the room. Again, he put his hand under her neck, head, back. Even more slowly, he began to raise her up. This time he ignored her sounds. Carefully, when she was at the proper height, he put the glass to her lips and tipped it toward her. Water dribbled down her chin, neck, chest, but some went into her mouth. She pulled back when she'd had enough and he gently lowered her. Finding some tissue, he mopped the spilled water from her body.

Then he tried once more. "Jaret, please listen and try to understand. I want to know who beat you up." He could not refer to the rape. "Can you describe him? Was he tall, short, fat, what? Please try and tell me, Jare."

"Mmmm," she said.

He whimpered again. Was it hopeless?

"Mih."

"What, Jare? What is it?" Maybe she wanted something else. What if she had to go to the bathroom?

"Miihd."

"Miihd?" he asked. "I don't understand, Jare. What do you want?"

She slowly rolled her head from side to side. "Miihd," she said more loudly. When Chris didn't respond she slammed at the bed with a closed fist. "Midd," she said again, clearer.

"Midd? What do you mean, Midd?" Mid, he thought. "Mid Summers? What about him? Oh, my

151

God! Jaret, listen, you don't mean Mid Summers did it, do you?"

"Yes," she whispered. "Mid did it."

"Je-sus," he said softly. Staring down at his sister's battered face, stunned by the name she'd just uttered, he did not hear the door open.

"What are you doing here?" a woman's voice snapped.

Chris whirled around. It was a nurse, a very large nurse.

"Who are you?" she demanded. "What do you want? Get away from that girl before I call the police."

She probably thought *he* was the one. "No," he said.

"Help," the nurse called. "Help!"

She turned toward the door and Chris, realizing the trouble he was in, took three giant steps, pushed her out of the way, flung open the door and started running down the hall. An orderly was coming toward him. Not wanting to do it, but feeling he had no other choice, he lowered his head. As the orderly and he were about to collide, he butted him out of the way and kept running. When he found the stairs he raced down, taking three and four at a time. Outside he continued to run until he neared town and knew he was safe. Soon he would find a hiding place where he could sit and think, recover. His plans had to be altered somewhat now that he knew one of his friends was the guy he had to get. But that was okay. Just fine.

"Are you all right, dear?" the big nurse asked.

Jaret nodded.

"Was that . . . was that the one?"

"Oh, no." Her mouth was so dry. "My brother."

"Your brother?"

"Yes. Water?"

The nurse held the glass to Jaret's lips as she drank. "Is there anything else you'd like, dear?"

Jaret shook her head.

"Just ring if you need anything."

When the nurse was gone Jaret closed her eyes all the way. It was hard for her to see anything anyway. She moved and groaned with pain. Everything ached, as though she'd been run over by a tank. She wondered what was broken. Surely her nose, as it was so difficult to breathe. She wondered if her eyes were black from the blow to her nose. Remembering that punch triggered her recall and everything began to come back, swimming through the murkiness of her mind to the shores of clarity. Part of her didn't want to remember. It was horrible enough to have gone through it the first time. But once the memories began she couldn't stop them. They were like a film

153

unrolling. She saw Mid's face, the hatred and anger, his fist coming toward her over and over. And she experienced anew the invasion of her body. That same feeling of helplessness overwhelmed her. She began to cry.

Her mind stumbled back to thoughts of Chris. Why had he been here? What was he going to do with the information she had given him? If she'd been more awake, alert, she'd have asked him, tried to temper any thoughts of retaliation he might have. How odd to think her little brother might want to get revenge for something that had happened to her. She never thought he gave her much thought these days. For a moment she was comforted by the idea of his caring. But, quickly, that feeling was replaced by fear. Fear for Chris, fear of more violence. When the police came should she mention Chris? Should she say she'd told him? It was so tiring. Tiring to think, feel, remember. But she was too agitated to sleep. There was nothing to do but wait.

20

Room 271 was crowded. Both Kay and Bert had insisted on being present with Chief Foster and Sergeant Leden when they questioned Jaret. Dr. Rosner was also there. The chief had refused to admit Peggy.

Foster pulled at one long earlobe. "Now, this isn't going to be pleasant, Jaret, but I have to ask you some questions, so to speak."

"I know," she said.

Kay, holding Jaret's hand, gave it a comforting squeeze.

"Now then," Foster said, "do you know the name of your attacker?"

"Yes."

Bert's hands involuntarily tightened into fists.

"Who was it?"

"Richard Summers," she said, "also known as Mid."

Kay's mouth dropped open slightly. He was a friend of Chris's, Zach Summers's brother. She looked at Bert as he, jolted, looked at her.

"You're sure of that?"

"Very sure."

"You know him personally, so to speak?"

"What d'you mean?"

"I mean, was he a friend?"

"A friend of my brother's."

"Oh?" Foster raised both bushy eyebrows as if he'd discovered a very important piece of information. "So then you knew him? He wasn't a stranger to you, so to speak?"

"No."

"Was he your boyfriend?" he asked suddenly, leaning over very close to her.

His tobacco breath was terrible and Jaret rolled her head away from him.

"Why are you turning away like that?" His tone was accusatory.

"What is this?" Bert said. "Why are you harrassing her?"

Foster stood up, slowly turned his hulking body toward Bert. "Mr. Tyler, I have allowed you to be

here during the questioning out of the goodness of
my heart and because, having a daughter of my own,
I know what you must be suffering. Howsoever, if this
continues, this outbursting, I'll have to ask the sergeant to escort you out." He turned back to Jaret, not
waiting for Bert to respond. "Now, young lady, was
this Richard Summers your boyfriend?"

"No." Jaret's eyes were closed.

"What were you doing in the woods with him
alone?"

"That's enough," Kay shouted. "Whose side are
you on?"

"Sergeant," Foster said, indicating Kay with a nod
of his head.

Leden, unmoving, flushed with discomfort. "Oh,
Chief, I don't think—"

"Sergeant Leden," the chief broke in, his tone
threatening, "would you please see the lady out?"

"I'm sorry, Mrs. Tyler." The sergeant's embarrassment prevented him from looking at Kay. "You'll
have to leave."

"The hell I will. You, Chief Foster, are harrassing
my daughter."

Dr. Rosner put a hand on Kay's arm. "You'll all
have to calm down or the questioning period will have
to terminate."

"Please," Jaret said. "It's okay, Mom. I can answer." She knew what Kay was reacting to, felt it her-

157

self, but she wanted to get this over with. "I wasn't *with* him in the woods. I was there by myself and he . . . he found me there."

"Why were you there alone?" Foster asked.

Bert simply couldn't contain himself. "Don't you think you ought to pick up the Summers boy?"

"You telling me my business, Mr. Tyler?"

"Maybe someone should."

"I cannot make an arrest until I know the details. There might be extenuating circumstances, so to speak."

"Look at her," Bert said. "What possible extenuating circumstances could there be?"

"Mr. Tyler, you don't understand. A case of rape and a case of assault are two different things."

"This is both," said Bert.

Foster smiled, nodded his head. "That, Mr. Tyler, is what I'm *trying* to determine."

His implication was clear. Obviously, Jaret had been brutally beaten; but perhaps the sexual act had *not* been rape.

Jaret broke the silence. "Chief, I wasn't a willing partner. He raped me."

"That so?" The chief shot a glance at Leden, who looked away. "Now then, when this boy found you *alone* in the woods, what were you doing?"

"I was lying on my blanket."

"Lying on a blanket," he repeated with astonishment.

158

Bert started to speak but Dr. Rosner stopped him with a hand on his arm.

"And what did you have on?" Foster asked.

"Now that's enough," said Kay.

"I ought to let you have it." Bert was ready to swing but Leden stepped between him and the chief.

"Mr. and Mrs. Tyler," said Foster, with exaggerated patience, "you are obstructing the wheels of justice, so to speak."

"And you're badgering my child," Kay said.

"I must look at all the possibilities."

"And you're saying that one of the probabilities is that Jaret was responsible for this? Is that right?"

"If she's innocent, Mrs. Tyler, then there's nothing to get so het up about."

"If?" Bert shouted.

"Mr. Tyler, *sir*," said the chief, full of condescension, "I have experience in these matters. A boy, a girl, a little kissing, maybe some petting, naturally the boy gets excited and then the girl says no. The poor boy goes crazy with frustration and—"

"I've heard everything I have to know," Kay said. "The *poor boy*? Oh, my God. It just makes me want to throw up."

Bert put his arm around Kay. "My daughter has told you who it was," he said. "And she has also told you that she was in the woods alone, that the Summers kid was not her boyfriend and that he beat and raped her. I think you have all the information you need." His tone was firm, deadly.

Foster started to say something, changed his mind and turned to go. Leden, flashing an apologetic smile at the Tylers, followed him.

Dr. Rosner shook his head. "Don't let it get to you, Bert."

"Why not?"

"You have a point. I think Jaret should rest now. You can take her home later this afternoon. There's nothing we can do for her here that loving parental care can't do."

Kay and Bert agreed, kissed Jaret good-bye and left her to get some sleep.

Chris, trembling, sat on the porch waiting for Mid to finish his breakfast, uncertain what he should do. Mid was two inches taller than he and had at least twenty-five pounds on him. Still, Chris didn't know if he would be able to control himself.

"Hiya, sport." Mid jabbed at Chris's arm with his fist.

Chris pulled away, brushed at the spot with his hand as though he'd been contaminated. He tried to smile, say hello. Nothing would come.

"You're up and at 'em early. What's the deal?" Mid danced around a porch post, shadowboxing. He didn't look at Chris. "Huh? How come? What's up?"

"Rape," Chris said solemnly. He hadn't intended

160

it to happen this way but something about Mid's behavior forced the word from his mouth.

Still Mid did not look at him. He kept sparring, dancing. "What?"

Chris grabbed Mid's arm. "Jaret," he said, speaking with difficulty, "Jaret was beaten and raped."

"No kidding?" Mid gave a long whistle. "Heavy."

"Shut up," Chris said. "Just shut up."

"What?"

"I know you did it, Mid," Chris squared off in front of him, his fists ready.

"You're crazy."

"She told me."

"Then she's crazy. I was in my room all yesterday afternoon."

"How'd you know when it happened?" He raised his fists slightly to waist level.

Mid began to stammer, face turning red.

"I know you did it, Mid, so there's no point saying you didn't."

"Get off my case, man. She's a queer. You try to lay this on me and I'll say that she does it with Peggy Danziger. I saw them."

Chris was incredulous. Could Mid really believe this threat would protect him? "Why did you do it?"

"Look at it this way, man. Now she knows what it's like with a guy. Whoever did it did the girl a favor. You don't want a dyke for a sister, do you?"

Chris swung. There was no question in his mind

161

that Mid had done it. Who else would talk that way? Mid ducked and started to laugh, sure Chris couldn't take him. What he didn't count on was Chris's anger and outrage. Mid was shocked when Chris tackled him and threw him to the ground. They rolled across the lawn, neither one hearing the police siren. Chris kneed Mid, who groaned and doubled over as Sergeant Leden jumped from his black-and-white.

Peggy saw Jaret for the first time around noon. Nothing she'd imagined was as bad as Jaret's bruised and battered face. "Oh, Cree Cree," she said, "you look just awful."

"Exactly what I wanted to hear."

"I'm sorry. I can't help it. I feel so guilty." Peggy began to cry. "It's all my fault. If only I hadn't left you alone, Jare."

The stinging memory of yesterday's fight returned to Jaret. Still, she knew Peggy wasn't responsible for what had happened. "Don't lay that trip on yourself, Peg. There was no way to know. Hindsight, sí, foresight, no." She attempted a smile which pulled at the front of her nose, hurting terribly. She moaned.

"Oh, babe," said Peggy.

"It only hurts when I breathe."

Peggy laughed.

"Anyway," said Jaret, "Foster's throwing the blame around like it's going out of style. Don't you try to get in on the act."

Jaret told her about the interview with the police chief. They discussed Foster, Mid, Claire.

Then Peggy said, "Jare, I have something to tell you. Last night while you were lying out there in the woods I was out with that gazinga. I'll never forgive myself." She covered her face with her hands, sobbing.

"What gazinga?"

"The McClinchie gazinga," she wailed. "I decided to get it over with."

"How was he?" Under the covers Jaret crossed her fingers.

"Just awful," Peggy bawled. "I couldn't relate to him at all. So *bor*-ing."

Jaret relaxed. "Come up for air," she said gently, stroking Peggy's hair.

"Do you forgive me?" She peeked at Jaret through her fingers.

"Course I do."

Quickly closing her fingers, Peggy said, "There's something else."

"What?"

"I kissed him."

Jaret felt a pang of jealousy. "And?"

Peggy took her hands from her face. "Have you ever kissed the outside of a cantaloupe?"

"No, but I've tried Wonder bread."

"That's it! Perfect."

163

They laughed. Jaret held her side.

"Oh, I can't keep making you laugh," Peggy said.

"No, please don't. Let's be serious."

The words were like some kind of cue for laughter. Jaret knew if she didn't stop she'd pass out from pain. "Okay, okay . . . listen."

"I'm listening."

"I'm serious now, really. There's something I didn't tell you about Mid. He's been watching us. He knows everything, and he said if I identified him he'd tell everyone about us."

"Oh." It was all Peggy could think to say.

"It was his ace in the hole, he said. He was sure I wouldn't want anyone to know, sure I'd never identify him because of it. Fool."

"Do you think he *will* tell?"

Jaret caressed her hand. "Yes, Peg, I do."

Slowly, Peggy stood and walked to the window, looked out over the green lawn.

"Peg?"

Peggy felt as though her life were ending, seeping away.

"Char? Can you bear it?"

Turning, Peggy looked at Jaret's ravaged face. Never had she felt more empty, more shallow in her life. Yet she felt impelled to be honest. "I don't know, Jare. I just don't know."

164

21

When Chief Foster appeared at the door, Bert tried to avoid letting him in. He found the man repulsive. But Foster claimed he had some important information and Bert felt he had no choice.

Kay was appalled to see the police chief sitting in her living room when she came down from tending Jaret. Bert saw the look on Kay's face.

"He says he has something important to tell us."

"Oh?" Kay ran splayed fingers through her hair.

"That's right," said Foster. "I'll get right to the point. Does the girl intend to press charges?"

"Of course," Bert said.

"Naturally," said Kay.

Foster shook his head, pressed his lips together and sighed. "I know how you feel. I can imagine if it was my little Sarah. But you really ought to think this thing over."

"Why? Is there any doubt that he did it?" Bert asked.

"None. He's confessed. Howsoever, there are complications." He took out a handkerchief and mopped his forehead. "This weather," he mumbled.

Kay and Bert exchanged glances. The air conditioning was cooling the room nicely.

Foster cleared his throat. "You see, the Summers boy claims the two girls . . . ah, your daughter and the Danziger girl, are ah . . ." He gave an odd, nervous laugh, wiped his hands with the handkerchief. "Ahh . . . intimate with each other."

Kay lit a cigarette, bit the inside of her lip. This was it.

"I beg your pardon," said Bert.

"Queer," said Foster. "That's what he claims. Says he's watched them . . . you know . . . together. Says that's why he decided to do it. They drove him to it."

Bert was on his feet. "I don't think I understand this," he said through pursed lips.

Kay reached out for him, touching his wrist with her fingers. He moved away, ignoring the contact.

Foster continued to twirl his handkerchief through

166

his hands. "This boy says that the girls are lesbians, Mr. Tyler. You know, lady lovers, so to speak."

"That's absurd," Bert said. "Ridiculous."

Kay couldn't let him go on. "No, Bert," she said. "It's not ridiculous. It's true."

Silence hung in the room like a shroud. Bert stared at his wife.

Kay broke the silence. "It's true, Bert. Jaret and Peggy have been having an affair for some time now."

Bert squinted at her as though seeing through a different perspective would make him understand better. "You're not serious?"

"Yes," she said. "I should have told you, I know. I . . ." She shrugged, helpless, recognizing the look of hurt and betrayal that crossed Bert's face, wishing she could hold him. When it became unbearable to look at him any longer, she turned to Foster. "I don't see what their relationship has to do with anything."

The chief jerked his head in surprise. "Well, now."

"I mean," Kay went on, "is their relationship supposed to be some sort of defense for him?"

"If I may say so, Mrs. Tyler, you seem to be taking perverted behavior in stride, so to speak."

She glanced at Bert. He looked undone. Back to Foster. "First of all I don't think it's perverted, but that's neither here nor there." She lit a fresh cigarette from the old one. "Secondly, no matter what their relationship is, it has absolutely nothing to do with

167

the fact that Jaret was beaten and raped. Does it?" she challenged him.

Foster shrugged his shoulders. "The Summers kid is gonna say that seeing them . . . you know, intimate and all . . . made him crazy."

"That's absurd," Bert said.

Kay saw that Bert would postpone his personal reactions and support her. She was relieved.

"You may think so, Mr. Tyler, but I guarantee you that this sort of deviant stuff doesn't go over too big in a nice little town like Gardener's Point." He sniffed.

"And rape does?" Bert said.

Foster ignored this. "The thing of it is that the Summers kid is gonna tell if you press charges. And there's something else. The Cross boy says he was intimate with your daughter. She wasn't a virgin," he said righteously.

"So what?" Kay was outraged. "What does that matter?"

"Well, well," Foster said with a mirthless chortle, "you certainly are modern parents. If I ever found out my Sarah wasn't a virgin I'd tan her hide."

Kay was furious that Foster had boxed her in this way.

Bert tried to help. "What Mrs. Tyler means is that whether Jaret is a virgin or not has nothing to do with the issue at hand." It was so strange to know this about his daughter, his little girl.

"Yes, that's right," said Kay.

Foster fanned himself with a magazine he'd picked up from the table. "Dry . . . that's what it is. Dry." He clucked his tongue several times.

Bert could see he was hinting for a drink but he'd be damned if he'd offer him anything.

Foster went on. "Let me put it to you this way. See, we have a hearing and the judge learns that your girl's not a virgin and on top of that she's a les. Well, he's not gonna think much of her morals. I'm just trying to give you some friendly advice."

"Are you telling me that this bum, this scum of the earth, is going to get away with what he did if we press charges?" Bert asked.

"Could very well be."

"Jesus," said Bert. "I can't be hearing right." He shook his head back and forth, staring down at the floor.

"The thing of it is," Foster said, "what I'm trying to bring out here is the Summers kid might get off and in the meantime your girl will have exposed herself, her private life, know what I mean? If I were in your shoes, I'd drop it."

"It's not our decision," Kay said.

"You want me to talk to her—put it to her straight?"

"No, we'll handle it," Bert said.

"I'm just trying to be helpful." The chief looked at them expectantly, waiting for their thanks. Getting none, he cleared his throat and lifted his hulking frame from the chair. "Well, you certainly are unusual parents. I guess it comes from living in the city."

"We've never lived in the city," Kay said.

"That so? Well, now."

Bert walked toward the door and Foster followed.

"If you're as smart as I think you are, you'll take my advice. If you go through with it there'll be a lot of mess for nothing. The boy is fifteen; even if he gets sent away, it won't be for long."

"Good night," Bert said pointedly.

"Your funeral," said Foster, going out the door. "Just being neighborly."

When Bert returned to the living room Kay was sitting on the couch, smoking, looking at him imploringly.

"I'm sorry, Bert," she said. "I really am."

"I don't understand why you didn't tell me."

"I guess I was trying to protect you. I didn't know if you could take it."

"Take it?" he said sitting on a footstool across the room.

"Bert, please try to understand. It wasn't easy for me either."

"But *you* could take it. You decided you were stronger than me, perhaps had more compassion and understanding. More intelligence maybe? Let's see, what else?"

"Don't," she said, feeling guilty.

170

"Why not, Kay? It's true, isn't it? You had no right to make a decision like that. I *am* Jaret's father and I have a right to know. *We* are parents. She has *two* parents, not one."

Kay knew he was right. "I'm sorry."

Bert could see she meant it. There was no point berating her any longer. Now he had to deal with his other feelings: feelings about Jaret having a sexual relationship with another girl. He wasn't sure what he thought, felt. He needed time to assimilate the information. But there were certain things he had to know.

"Is it our fault?" he asked. "Mine? Did I make her afraid of men or something?"

"No, Bert. It's not like that."

"Is it a phase, Kay?" He tried to sound hopeful.

"I don't think so."

"What are we going to do?"

"We're going to love her," Kay said firmly. "That's what we're going to do."

Jaret awoke abruptly. She'd been dreaming about Mid again. The woods, the rape. She supposed that was to be expected. After all, it had only been a little more than forty-eight hours.

Lying in the semidarkness of her room, she tried to focus on her feelings about Mid. Did she hate him? Want him dead? Past discussion of rapists came floating back to her. "They're sick men." "They need to be hospitalized, not jailed." "We should feel sorry for them." Did she believe it? *Was* Mid sick? Or was he just bad? Bad? Jaret wasn't even sure what that meant. And what difference did it make whether he was bad or sick? Did that really have any bearing on what she felt? His problems were his. Hers were hers. She'd been raped by this boy and she was beginning to feel angry. She'd had no choice about what had happened to her. She had been taken against her will. Violated. Attacked. Assaulted. Abused. And she had been beaten.

Jaret could feel rage moving through her body, causing it to shake. How dare anyone do that to her? Who did he think he was? And to threaten her with the revelation of her affair with Peggy. The pig! Let him say what he wanted; it made no difference to her. But what about Peggy? She shook the thought away. Not even Peggy could change things; no one could, now. It was done. If he made her go to court, she'd go. And if it all came out there, well, that was too bad. She'd never felt such hatred, and it made her uneasy. But when she saw his face in her mind, remembered his breath on her neck, once again endured his blows her uneasiness dissipated. Mid Summers was going to be punished, no matter what it took, no matter whom it hurt. That was firm.

22

When Zach heard about the rape he cried. After Bianca told him he went to the door of his shop, turned the CLOSED sign outward and pulled down the green shade, walked back behind the counter, sat down on the stool, put his head on his arms and cried.

Bianca didn't know what to do. She'd never seen Zach, or any grown man, cry, and she was shocked, although she hated herself for feeling that way. She'd thought she was liberated enough to allow men the same emotions as women. Her shock quickly passed, however, and soon she was behind the counter comforting Zach.

When he finished she asked if he was crying for

Jaret or Mid.

"Both," he said. Zach had been aware for some time that his brother was disturbed, and had urged his parents, to no avail, to get Mid some help.

"What will happen?" Bianca asked, thumping Zach's back in her version of a pat.

"I don't know," he said. "I'm not sure. I know you're Jaret's friend. Will this change anything between us?"

"Well, you didn't do it!" Bianca was horrified.

But a week later, after Mid had been released on bail, as they sat in Zach's store once again, Bianca said, "I cannot believe that your brother is act-u-ally going to plead not guilty. It's an outrage."

Zach was embarrassed by the whole thing. He'd tried to talk Mid out of using the lesbian relationship as part of his defense but Mid had laughed at him. And Mid's lawyer said it just might work. Zach found it disgusting, cheap. But he was also uncomfortable about discovering Jaret and Peggy were lesbians. He didn't know what to make of it, what to think.

Bianca went on. "It seems to me, dar-ling, that you could do something."

"You know I've tried. I hate the whole business." He looked at her sheepishly. "I think you should know he's seeing a reporter from *The Press* today."

Bianca stiffened. "And *what* does that mean?"

"Look, Bianca, I tried to stop it but there was

174

nothing . . . He's going to tell about Jaret and Peggy."

She got off the stool slowly, picked up her handbag, straightened her spine and, standing at her full height, said, "I must go to my friends."

He watched her leave, saying nothing. In his heart Zach knew his love affair with Bianca was coming to a close. It would be too much for her, this split between friends and lover, as it was for him between lover and family. Loyalty would divide them. He felt sad and helpless.

Accused Rapist Claims Victim's Unnatural Relationship Responsible

Tom Danziger didn't die when he heard about Peggy and Jaret. He didn't even have a nervous collapse.

"No, I haven't read it," he said to his sister, Paula, on the phone.

"Well, are you sitting down?" Paula asked.

He was not but said he was.

"It says that Peggy and Jaret are lesbians. Can you believe that?"

"Yes," he said calmly.

"What do you mean *Yes?*"

"I mean, yes, I can believe it." He realized that

175

knowledge of their relationship had been with him for some time. He simply hadn't allowed it to surface.

"You're not telling me that you knew this, are you?"

Tom didn't want to discuss this with Paula, or anyone, until he had had time to think. "I have a patient, Paula. I'll call you back later."

"I think it's disgusting, Tom. I think you should sue."

"I'll talk to you later." He hung up. His first patient wasn't due for fifteen minutes.

Peggy and Jaret. Lovers. No, it wasn't a surprise. He hadn't really looked at it but had felt it pass through his mind like something on its way to somewhere else. Obviously, he had not *wanted* to think about it, deal with it. He'd been absorbed instead with trying to heal his own wounds and had not looked at his younger daughter honestly. But now it was a reality, in black and white apparently, for all to see, know, react to. What did he feel about it? He said the word. Lesbian. My daughter is a lesbian. He didn't like it; it wasn't comfortable. He imagined the reactions of his colleagues at the hospital, saw their faces, heard the remarks behind his back. He squirmed in his chair, clucked his tongue.

What a phony liberal you are, he thought. Always preaching live and let live; always railing against forces that would deny *anyone's* civil rights. Was this all that it really amounted to, all his huffing and puffing? That it was all right for others to be homosexual but not his own?

Of course, maybe it wasn't even true. Why was he so quick to believe the ravings of a confessed rapist? Because he *knew*. Still, it probably was just a passing thing. A phase. Didn't all little girls go through a homosexual phase? Embarrassed by this ridiculous rationalization, Tom lit a cigarette. Peggy was not a little girl, by any stretch of the imagination. But she *had* lost her mother and perhaps this was simply some kind of temporary substitution. Yes, that was probably it. He would make an appointment for her with Dr. Crawford, the hospital's resident psychiatrist. A few sessions and this would be straightened out. Peggy would be herself again before she started college.

But meanwhile. Meanwhile the accusation was in the papers. How would they deal with it? The first thing he'd do was ask Peggy if it was true. Then they would go from there. The intercom on his desk buzzed. He flicked the switch. "Yes?"

"Mrs. Jaffe, your first appointment this morning, has canceled. So have Mr. Dorman and Alice Rosenfelt. They didn't give any reasons and they didn't make any future appointments."

He thanked his receptionist, sat back in his chair and smiled ruefully. So that's the way it's going to be, he thought. Well, he'd been thinking of moving anyway.

When the paper came Jaret was alone in the house. Peggy wasn't with her because they had broken up. After reading the story Jaret lay on her bed and cried. Peggy had been right; it was going to be awful. Still, Jaret knew she couldn't have done anything else. Once again, she went over that final day with Peggy.

"What good will it do, Cree Cree?" Peggy had pleaded. "Since when are you into an eye for an eye?"

"Since I was raped."

"Don't you care about me?"

"Of course I do," Jaret said. "You just don't understand."

"What about the price you'll pay?"

"The price *you'll* pay, you mean."

"Okay. Right." Peggy began to pace. "I can't take it, Jare. And besides, my father will die."

"No, he won't. My father didn't and my mother and I thought he'd freak out or something."

"Your father's different. I mean, he's not a doctor. It'll wreck his career. You know what a bummer that'd be if I was responsible for wrecking his career?"

"Come off it, Peg. Maybe he'll lose a few patients

178

but he'll get others." Jaret ran her tongue over her bottom lip. It barely hurt anymore. She felt the split healing over.

"He'll die of embarrassment."

"No, he won't. Look, it wasn't exactly a breeze for my father, but I made him understand that you made me very happy and that I wasn't some weirdo, all sick and miserable with guilt, and that it had nothing to do with him. You know what he said? He said, Who could be against a happy relationship? See? It's all in how you present it. Now when you tell your father . . ."

"Tell him? Are you freaking or what?" Peggy threw a small pillow at the wall.

"You want him to find out in court? He probably knows anyway."

"He doesn't," Peggy said defensively. She sat down next to Jaret and put an arm around her. "Don't do it, Cree."

"I have to."

Peggy jumped up. "Maybe you don't give a gazinga if people think you're a . . . a queer, but I do."

The words stung. Raising her chin slightly, Jaret said dramatically, "That's the other reason I'm doing it. It's time to come out of the closet."

"Now I know you're freaking."

"The more people who come out of the closet, the less it'll be an issue," she said, full of self-importance.

179

What had started as a response to Peggy's use of the word queer was becoming a polemic. Enthusiastically, Jaret went on. "I *am* a lesbian, Peg, and I don't intend to live the rest of my life sneaking around pretending to be something I'm not. It's my duty to go to court and declare myself. I have no choice."

"Who are you? Bianca?"

Jaret came back to earth. She believed much of what she'd said, but that wasn't why she was fighting Mid Summers. "I hate him," she said evenly.

"Vengeance is not yours," said Peggy.

"Oh, yes it is."

"You're selfish."

"So are you."

They stared at each other a long time. Finally, Peggy broke the silence.

"Okay. Okay, Jaret. I didn't want to have to stoop to this but I see there's no other way to reach you. You're inhuman. If you do this, if you press those humungus charges and that creep tells about us, I'll never see you again."

The words rang in the air like tolling bells. There was a moment when Jaret wavered. The moment passed.

She had refused and Peggy had left her alone. Forever. Now Jaret flung the newspaper across the room. Well, she'd made her bed and now she was lying in it. But she really hadn't had a choice. It would have been cowardly to do anything else. And besides, how could she expect to become a lawyer if she couldn't even press charges in an open-and-shut case?

But there were times when she didn't think she could survive without Peggy. It was as though her insides were trickling away. She went to her desk and picked up the poem she'd found the night before and read it again.

You entered in my daily scheme of living
So stealthily I did not know that Life
Had caught our threads together in weaving.

And when I knew, I tried too late to stop her.
Already you were woven in my soul,
And when I tore you out
                It raveled. . . .

Tears stained Jaret's cheeks as she put the poem back in its place. It didn't matter if every line applied or not. It still got to her, especially the last two lines. Raveled. Yes. Shredded. Torn. Peggy had become such a part of her she now felt incomplete.

She turned from her desk and saw that Chris was standing in the doorway.

"Hi," he said.

"Hi."

"I saw the paper down at the Hive."

181

"Come on in." She wiped away her tears with her sleeve.

Chris flopped across the bed, leaned on an elbow. "It stinks," he said.

She nodded. "At least I have you and Mom and Dad."

"Did Peggy fink out on you?" he asked.

"Chris, you know, we never talked about what you did that day. Going after Mid like that."

"What's to talk about?"

"Why'd you do it?"

"What d'you mean? He hurt you, I wanted to hurt him. Simple." He looked past her shoulder.

"Is that the only reason?"

"Sure, what else?"

"I don't know." She touched his hand. "Are you angry with me? Do you hate me?"

He was shocked, sat up. "Me? Hate *you*? No. I thought . . . I mean, wow . . . I thought *you* hated me."

"Why?" she asked, dumbfounded.

"Well, I'm a . . . a guy."

"I don't hate men, Chris."

"You don't? Then how come . . . ? I mean, how come you're a . . . ?"

"A lesbian? It's not such a terrible word. I'm not sure why but it definitely isn't because I hate men."

"Not even after what happened?"

182

"No. I'm angry at him, Mid, but not all men. Not you."

"I thought for sure"—he cleared his throat—"lesbians hated men."

"Well, we don't. But what's that got to do with you going after Mid? And don't tell me it was just because he hurt me because I won't buy it."

Chris stood up, shuffled back and forth at the end of the bed. Then he said, "I thought if you saw a guy do something good, you know, kind of brave . . . well, I thought maybe you wouldn't think all guys were so bad."

"Oh, Chris." Jaret loved him more then than she ever had.

"I didn't know you didn't think we were all turkeys. I could have saved myself a few lumps." He grinned at her.

"You mean you're sorry you stood up for me?"

Chris looked her straight in the eyes. "Jaret, all I got to say to that is: Does a chicken have lips?"

She laughed and wanted to hug him but he was out the door before she had a chance.

23

Claire insisted she be in on the talk and Tom, as always, deferred to her wishes.

"So you knew about it all along?" he said to Claire.

"I couldn't tell you, Daddy. You were upset enough."

He nodded. He couldn't blame Claire for his own failure to deal with things. To Peggy he said, "Didn't you know it would appear in the paper? Couldn't you have given me a little warning?"

"If I could have I would," she said, not looking at him. "Would it really have made such a difference?"

He wasn't sure. Anyway, that was not the issue

at hand. "I made an appointment for you with Dr. Crawford."

Peggy's head snapped up. "Why? Do you think I'm crazy?"

"Of course not. You know better than that. People don't see psychiatrists only because they're crazy. I just think you're a bit disturbed. After all, you *did* lose your mother. I should have thought of it sooner."

"Disturbed because of . . . of Jaret and me, you mean."

"Well, what else?" said Claire. "It's not normal, as I've told you time and again."

"Shut up, Claire."

"Well, it's not."

"Please," Tom said.

"I don't have to see Dr. Crawford. It's over. Me and Jaret, I mean."

"Oh? How come?" Tom's fingers made a crimp in his chin.

"Thank God for small favors," Claire said. "You should still see Dr. Crawford though. It could happen again. It's only a symptom, after all."

Peggy glared at her. "What do you know?"

"I am *majoring* in psychology, in case you've forgotten."

"Who could forget?"

"What happened with you and Jaret?" Tom interrupted.

185

"Nothing happened. It's just over, that's all."
Peggy felt like crying.

"Things end for a reason," Tom said gently, noting
the look on his daughter's face.

If Claire hadn't been there, Peggy might have
explained; as it was, all she could do was shrug her
shoulders.

"Could you at least tell me who ended it?" Tom
asked.

"I did." Oh, Jaret, she thought. I miss you so.

"I get the impression, Peggy, that you aren't comfortable with lesbianism. Is that correct?"

Slowly, she nodded.

"So you finally admit it," Claire said.

"Claire, please," said Tom. "This is hard enough
for all of us." He took a gamble. "But you still care
for Jaret, don't you?"

Peggy's control was shattered. "Oh, Daddy," she
said and burst into tears.

Tom took her in his arms as she sobbed against his
chest. Claire left the room. When she could speak
again, Peggy told him everything.

"You needn't have worried about me," he said,
stroking her hair.

"Well, how do you feel about it?"

He couldn't lie. "I find it . . . disturbing. I'm
afraid for you. I want you to be happy—have a
normal life. I don't know what the hell a normal

life is, but what I mean, Peg, is that life is tough enough without stacking the deck. If you were in love with a black boy I'd feel the same way. It's asking for trouble, that's all."

"Are you horrified?" she asked tentatively.

Was he? Of course not. That was much too strong. Actually, Tom realized, sex between two girls, two women, just didn't seem all that important to him. "No, I'm not horrified, Peggy. As a matter of fact, I think it's hard for me to take lesbianism very seriously."

She was shocked. "That's very chauvinistic."

"Is it?"

"Sure." She wished Jaret were here. She was so much better at explaining these things, always remaining calm and intelligent while Peggy got emotional, inarticulate. She took a stab at it anyway. "What you're saying, Daddy, is that women are not really sexual beings."

"Hardly." Tom didn't like this turn in the conversation. "Does it horrify you?" he asked.

She thought about making love with Jaret and how beautiful it was when they were together. "No, it doesn't. What horrifies me is what other people think. That's why I didn't want Jaret to make it public. You know how people are."

Tom thought of the seven patients who had canceled that day. "That's exactly what I'm afraid of for

187

you. That's what I meant about life being hard enough. I think you should see Dr. Crawford. Unless you work it out it might come up again. You know, with someone else."

Peggy shook her head. "Never." It was Jaret, only Jaret. Still, she had to admit that the thought of being with a man didn't appeal to her. Maybe she should see someone. Maybe it would help. "All right, I'll see him."

"Good. Now in the meantime don't go worrying about me. I'll be just fine. Just one thing. If anyone asks me directly, should I deny it?"

"How can you? Jaret's going to court. She'll admit to it."

"I see." So he was going to have to face it head on. Well, so what? It might be rough going for a while but, eventually, it would all blow over, become a thing of the past. And, basically, his daughter was a heterosexual. Of that he was sure. Thank God!

When Peggy glanced into Claire's room as she passed, she saw her sister throwing clothes into a suitcase.

"What are you doing?" Peggy asked.

"Building a bridge. What does it look like?"

"Going somewhere?"

"Yes. I am leaving this disgusting house. Forever."

"Where are you going?"

"That's none of your business," Claire said, pulling out a drawer. "I just don't intend to hang around here and be dragged down in the mud. You're sick and he's an ingrate. I've had it."

"You're very understanding for a psychology major."

"Shove it."

"Charming."

Claire whirled around, facing Peggy. "You just think you can get away with anything, don't you?"

"I'm not trying to *get away* with anything," Peggy said.

"You make me sick."

"So you've said. And said."

"And I'll keep on saying it. You have no regard for anyone else. I told you this would happen." She emptied a sock drawer onto the bed.

"There was nothing I could do, Claire. It's Jaret's gazinga."

"Really?"

"I mean, there was nothing I could do to stop her from pressing charges. Do you think I dig this?"

Claire pushed back her glasses. "How should I know what someone like you likes or doesn't. You are a selfish, self-involved brat with an inflated ego. I may not have had looks but at least I had the reputation of being a decent person. Now that's gone. Guilt by association."

"That's ridiculous," Peggy said, feeling guilt of her own.

"Is it? This afternoon Marge Allen called to break a theater date we had for next week. It was a very lame excuse and when I said I'd call her she said she was going to be very busy for the rest of the summer."

"I'm sorry," Peggy said. She was.

"You should have thought of sorry when you started your sordid affair."

"It is . . . was not sordid."

"It is beyond me," Claire said, walking toward her, "why, if you were going to be a dyke, you had to get the looks."

"Have you ever thought of plastic surgery?" Peggy said angrily.

Claire slapped her across the face and Peggy slapped back. They stood, squared off, glaring at one another.

Quietly, controlled, Claire spoke. "I loathe you and I never want to see you again. Now get out of my room."

Within an hour Claire had left. She told her father that she would be staying at a friend's in New York City until school began and gave him the address in case of an emergency. She also warned him not to use it unless it was absolutely essential. She said that she never wanted to see him and Peggy again and that they could both rot in hell for all she cared.

Tom tried to stop her but it was no use. She was, after all, a grown woman. He hoped she would change her mind after some time passed; he knew he would try to reason with her at a later date. But for now he could do nothing but let her go. After she left, Peggy was numb with guilt. Tom grieved for them all.

24

The hearing was scheduled for November tenth. Jaret knew Mid's lawyer had had it postponed, hoping that maybe she wouldn't show up. But Jaret was determined, no matter what was going on at college, to come back for the hearing. Too much had happened to give it all up now. And she would win. Even in Gardener's Point, there was no way Mid could win. She would be smeared, and Peggy along with her, but Mid Summers would be punished!

Dropping the charges now wouldn't help those who were already hurt. It was far too late for that. They were like battle casualties. What good would it do them if an armistice were suddenly declared?

192

Jaret's trunk had been sent on ahead to Radcliffe and now she was packing her last suitcase. Nothing was ever as you imagined it, planned it. Peggy was right. You could never write the script. There was no point in living more than one day at a time. Here she was, getting ready for the biggest moment of her life, and she felt miserable. She sat down on her bed, overcome with guilt. Questions of selfishness still plagued her. Even though Kay had assured her that she was doing the right thing by going to court, Jaret sometimes wondered if the end *did* justify the means. The body count was very high.

Bianca and Zach, for instance.

"I sim-ply cannot continue to see a man who is blinded by familial ties. I find it a dread-ful trait," Bianca had said.

"I think it's kind of admirable," said Jaret.

"You are beyond comprehension. In some instances, that kind of loyalty *would* be admirable; not in this one. If there were any question of Mid's guilt I could, perhaps, understand it. But not this. Oh no, not this, oh Lord!" She put her hand, palm out, to her forehead.

Jaret thought of telling her that was a very old-fashioned gesture but decided to skip it. "So you're breaking up, then?"

"Broken up. Past tense, my dear. The deed is done. Somehow," she said, looking off into space, "I'll survive."

193

And Jaret agreed that she would.

Later, Kay pointed out to Jaret that Bianca was probably glad Zach had chosen to stand by his brother so that she could gracefully, and dramatically, extricate herself. Had he not done so, she'd have had no excuse for leaving him and would have remained the sweetheart of the man whose brother had raped her friend, an uncomfortable position to hold.

Even so, Jaret could not help feeling some guilt about their breakup. It was dumb, she knew. It wasn't her fault that she'd been raped, although many people would have liked her to believe it was. Like Chief Foster and half of Gardener's Point, for instance. Jaret heard bits and pieces of things and knew some people blamed her simply because she was female. She must have seduced Mid, led him on, by her dress, her manner, her actions. This attitude was outrageous and archaic but then so was Gardener's Point. As for her lesbianism, that was another matter. Those who labeled her seductress simply couldn't deal with her as a lesbian. Generally, people fell into two camps: the ones who thought of her as *whore* and those who thought of her as *queer*. It was when Jaret concentrated on these people that she lost her guilt and strengthened her resolve to fight Mid Summers in court.

Now she looked in the mirror, touched the slight bump on her nose that would be there forever, re-

194

minding her. Secretly, Jaret didn't mind it; she felt it gave her character. Resuming her packing, she lovingly placed in the suitcase a green turtleneck Peggy had given her for her birthday.

It was a month since they'd seen each other. Again Jaret felt the familiar ache. Losing Peggy was, of course, the worst thing that had happened since the rape. Jaret had received only one communication from her. Oh, how she'd trembled as she'd held Peggy's letter in her hand, frightened to open it, frightened not to. It was, she knew, an apology. A letter asking for forgiveness. She could have yelped with joy. Then she had opened it.

Dear Jaret,

Under separate cover I have sent you all your letters. I think it would be a mistake for us to keep them; like hanging on to souvenirs. I hope you will return mine soon.

I also hope this letter finds you feeling better.
Best,
Peg

Jaret had wept hurt and angry tears. Peggy's letters were all she had of better days, but there was no way she could deny the request. She returned them im-

195

mediately and when her own letters arrived she read them through once, crying the whole time, then ceremoniously burned them in the back yard.

When Jaret heard Peggy was seeing a psychiatrist, it made her sad. She'd never known Peggy found their relationship upsetting enough to have to go into therapy. And it made her wonder if Peggy had ever loved her at all. When Jaret also heard that Claire had left home and that Tom had put his house and practice up for sale, she knew how lucky she was. Kay and Bert and Chris had stood their ground, backed her one hundred percent. Her brother and father coming through the way they had had been a wonderful surprise. Kay, of course, had always supported her. Jaret remembered a day in the first grade when she had come home in tears because her teacher, Mrs. Ackroyd, had dashed her hopes of becoming a garbage collector.

"You can be anything you want, kid," Kay had said. "You tell Mrs. Ackroyd that there are no limitations in this house."

And it had been the same last night when Kay came into her room to say good night; in a sense, to say good-bye.

"I'm gonna miss you, kid." She straddled a chair, took her portable ashtray from her pocket, lit a cigarette.

"You going to try to give it up this year, Mom?"

"I'll try. I promise." Kay waved the smoke away. "Are you scared?"

"A little. New things are always scary but, oh, wow, after this summer . . ."

"Gotcha. Jaret, I hope you know how proud I am of you."

"Same here, Mom."

"I didn't do anything. You did. You withstood . . . well, I don't have to tell you."

"But so did you. And I get to go away. You all still have to live here."

"Jare, I really knew who my friends were before this thing happened. Nothing much changed. So I get the fisheye from the butcher. Hey, that's funny."

They laughed, reaching out to touch each other. Kay got up from the chair and sat next to Jaret on her bed. "Please, Jare, I don't want you worrying about us. We'll be fine. Even Chris. He's a good kid, you know."

"I *do* know."

"How do you feel now? It's almost six weeks since it happened. I worry about what's going on in your head."

"I'm okay. I feel angry and then guilty and then sad and, oh, everything, I guess. But most of the time I know I'm doing the right thing. I promised you, Mom, if it starts to get to me at school, I'll see a doctor."

197

"Good." Kay ran a hand over Jaret's hair, kissed her cheek.

"I want to ask *you* something, Mom. Does it bother you that you'll never have any grandchildren from me?"

Kay smiled. "No. First of all, I'll probably have a couple from Chris. But even if I don't, so what? Listen, kid, anybody can be a grandmother but not anybody can be the mother of a brave, independent lesbian who's also a lawyer."

"I'm not a lawyer yet."

"Yeah, but you will be. I have no doubts. You'll be anything you want to be, Jaret. You already are, thank God."

And there it was. Her mother's gift. She hoped she could always keep it in the front of her mind. She sighed, touched the green turtleneck and turned back to the dresser, glancing in the mirror. She jumped, whirled around.

"Hi, Jare," Peggy said.

"What are you doing here?" She hoped she wouldn't have heart failure.

"I had to see you."

Jaret looked at her watch. "I have an hour and a half before I have to go." She sounded testy and wondered why she was acting this way. Fear?

"Should I leave?"

Was it to be a game, a test? "Oh, Peggy, please. I

198

don't know . . . What do you . . . ? Oh, this is the pits."

"Not at all the way you'd imagined, huh? Me either." She smiled, took a small step into the room.

Gently, Jaret said, "Believe it or not I never imagined it. I really thought I'd never see you again."

"Can I come in, Jare?"

"Sure." Quickly she moved the suitcase to the floor, pushed aside some clothes and made a space for Peggy to sit. She took the chair. "I thought you'd left for Smith."

"Tomorrow. I had my dates wrong." She pushed a strand of blond hair from her face.

"And here I was imagining you on the train, getting there, meeting new people. . . ." Jaret flushed, realizing she'd given away how much she missed her, cared still. Well, so what? It *wasn't* a game.

Peggy pressed her lips together, looked down at her sneakers. "It's been a humungus month without you, Jaret."

Jaret realized she had been holding her breath. Trying to breathe normally, she said, "Me too. I mean humungus for me too."

Raising her head, Peggy's eyes sought Jaret's. "I've been seeing Dr. Crawford."

"I know."

Peggy nodded, realizing that Jaret *would* know. "He's helped me, Jare."

"Good. I'm glad." Jaret wondered if Peggy had come to tell her she was "cured" and that Jaret could be too.

"I learned a lot about myself. It's too long and too hard to explain now."

Now? A small sputter of hope flared inside Jaret.

"But the important thing is . . . the important thing is that I love you. At least it's important to me."

"Oh, wow, Peg. Did you just find that out today?" she said, laughing. "I mean, you cut it awfully close."

Peggy smiled. "You're not going to believe this but the answer is yes. I mean, *really* found out. I thought of you leaving, on the train and all that, and suddenly . . . Oh, God, I sound like a dumb movie, but it's true. . . . *Suddenly* I realized how much I'd missed you, loved you, and that nothing anybody else thought or did mattered. The only thing that mattered was you and me."

"Oh, Peg."

"It's not too late, is it, Cree?"

"Too late?"

"Too late for us?" She let Jaret see her crossed fingers.

"No, it's not too late. But, Peg, nothing has changed. I'm still going through with the trial."

"I know." Peggy leaned into the pillows.

"Will you be able to stand it?"

200

"I don't know. That's the truth. The trouble is I still do care what people think but I have to try not to. Oh, Jare, I don't want to spend the rest of my life being what other people want me to be."

Jaret crossed to the bed and sat down next to her. "Do you know what you want to be?" she asked softly, taking Peggy's hand.

"You mean sexually?"

Jaret nodded.

"I only know that I love you and that I want to be with you now. But that's the way I am about everything. I'm not you, so sure and definite about everything. I mean, you've known you wanted to be a lawyer since you were six."

"Seven. At six it was a garbage collector."

"I don't know what I want to do with my life in any way."

"You don't have to. Now is the only thing that counts, to quote a friend."

"I can't make you any promises." Peggy touched her cheek.

"Neither can I, Char."

Looking into each other's eyes, a moment passed and then they glided easily into one another's arms, holding, loving.

"I'm so sorry, Jaret," Peggy whispered.

"Don't."

"I'm proud of you. Scared to death but, nevertheless, proud. You've got a lot of gazinga!"

"I think," Jaret said, "you have more gazinga than you know."

They held each other tightly, knowing the future held many surprises, that nothing was guaranteed. And so what if happy endings didn't exist? Happy moments did.